I0619370

TASTE FOR COFFEE

A TASTE FOR LOVE NOVELLA

FRANCINE BEATON

ALSO BY FRANCINE BEATON

For my Husband and Daughter

PROLOGUE

The weather was as sombre as the atmosphere. The wind howled around the corners of the small country church, sweeping the rain against their clothes and faces. The umbrella Kirsty held over Joe didn't provide enough shelter.

Not that her grandfather noticed. His eyes remained on the casket. Though her own heart was breaking about the loss of her beloved godfather, she could only imagine how Joe must suffer, burying his best friend.

Kirsty huddled closer to him, more in comfort than because of the weather.

Her eyes drifted over the people assembled in the cemetery next to the Cramond Parish church. There was a divide more significant than the grave between them. Other than their lawyer, Kirsty had never met the people on the other side of the grave. Of course, several often appeared in papers or on television.

Except for the Young siblings. They stood in the middle of the crowd, directly opposite Kirsty and her grandfather. She caught glimpses of them earlier in the church, but now she saw them clearly for the first time. Even if she hadn't known about them, she would've recognised the man in the middle as Drew's son. He had a similar strong built as his parent, but the similarities didn't end there. Kirsty had seen photographs of Drew in his younger years and the man standing across from her was a mirror image of that man. She didn't have to wonder how he would look in his fifties and sixties.

He was gorgeous. Kirsty's heart fluttered as she kept her eyes on him throughout the service.

He raised his eyes from the casket. He stared straight at Kirsty, but she doubted he saw anything. If he did, it might be memories of the father they were saying goodbye to today. She read the sheer and utter desolation in his eyes, shimmering in the grey light of the day. The muscles of his jaw and throat worked hard to control his emotions.

Kirsty wished she could take away the grief etched on his face. It was a pain every person dealt with differently. Realising the pain for what it was, it didn't take away the fact she would have loved to be the person who consoled and supported Iain Young.

Kirsty made a shocking discovery. She lost her heart to a man who didn't know she even existed, at a funeral of all places.

How foolish was that?

1

Iain glared in exasperation at the three people sitting in front of him.

"Don't tell me that none of you can convince the woman to move? For goodness sake, she won't get a better offer. Why is she so freaking obstinate?"

The Property Maintenance Manager, Walter Mackay, shrugged. "*Aye*, but Miss Brown said she has a valid lease and intends to keep it."

Iain ignored his irritation aimed at Mackay who was leaning back in his chair. Iain didn't like Mackay, although he couldn't put his finger on the reason for his dislike yet. Maybe it was because Mackay was too slick. Iain made a mental note to keep an eye on him.

Turning away, he barked at his brother Graeme, "You. You're the lawyer. Could you not convince the woman to end her lease earlier?"

Graeme shook his head, "I tried. I threw everything I had at her, but she refused to budge. I even threatened to take her to court to contest the validity of the lease. She only smiled and gave me her lawyer's card."

Iain sighed. "Don't tell me. Someone we're supposed to know?"

Graeme nodded, "None other than Dougie Munroe."

Iain cursed. With Dougie Munroe involved and Kirstine Brown as confident as Graeme imitated, they didn't stand a chance. Dougie, or Dougal Munroe, was one of their father's oldest friends and one of the sharpest lawyers Iain knew. Dougie would have covered all the bases.

Iain sighed, shoving his hands through his already messy hair. "Aileen?"

His sister, the Vice-President: Assets and Marketing for Young Incorporated also shook her head. "Kirstine Brown is adamant. I've even tried offering her other lease options, but she refused. Miss Brown said Joe's Coffee House had been there for over twenty years. If it were up to her, Joe's would stay right where it was."

Aileen smirked. "She added that both our father and her grandfather would turn in their graves if you put a chain restaurant there."

Aileen frowned, "Did you guys know that Dad had been a regular at Joe's? There's even a photo in the restaurant of him and Joe at the opening over twenty years ago."

Both brothers denied it. Hell, Iain had never even heard of the building or Joe Brown and his granddaughter before this. His father had kept a part of his life hidden from his children. Iain wondered about that. Anyway, it was no use speculating about it now. His problem was that building his father left to Iain. Although Young's administrate it, it didn't form part of Young's portfolio.

Iain threw his pen so hard on the table in frustration that it bounced off and onto the carpet. He scowled at it and bent to pick it up while considering his options.

He could either get rid of the building or re-develop it. That was where his problem lay. He couldn't do either if he couldn't get rid of Joe's. Iain might have no other choice than confronting Miss Brown himself.

Iain already had to postpone his plans when the owner of Joe's had passed away in early January. There was a process to follow to register Joe's in the name of Joe Brown's only heir so Iain couldn't do anything. He had to bide his time and wait, frustration mounting by the day.

Since the completion of the process, Iain first sent Mackay to negotiate. Graeme and Aileen both tried. None of them succeeded.

Now, because they had failed, he had to step in himself. He scowled again. He didn't have time to deal with one tenant, especially not one as obstinate as this one was.

Iain concluded the meeting, and as soon as they left the office, he pulled the folder closer. He needed to prepare. He refused to back down.

KIRSTY RECOGNISED the man the moment he walked into Joe's and she shivered.

You couldn't help but notice Iain Young. He looked a lot like his father, Drew. At six-foot-three and well-muscled, he was an impressive man. If you knew none better, you would have thought he was a professional athlete. He had the build for it.

That wasn't what made Iain stand out from the crowd nor was it those arresting blue eyes. It was far more than that. Iain Young had a presence, an intensity about him that made Kirsty uncomfortable.

She had expected him, but not so soon.

If ever a man looked like trouble, he was now standing at the entrance of Joe's Coffee House. He surveyed the shop with an almost disdainful expression on his face and his hands on his hips. His hands pushed his coat and suit jacket open, revealing a muscled, sculpted chest underneath a crisp white shirt.

The expression on his face made Kirsty's hackles rise. There was nothing wrong with Joe's. Well, Joe's might need a lick of paint, but apart from that, there was nothing wrong with it. The painting was a project on the following year's to-do list. Losing Joe had already been traumatic. She first wanted to find her feet running Joe's without her grandfather's guidance before she made any significant changes.

Gorgeous or not, that unhappy customer could turn around and go back to where he came from. Her regulars loved Joe's, and they were more important than a city boy who only dropped in here to stir trouble.

Iain hadn't moved. He was still scanning the crowd inside the restaurant as if he was searching for someone. Kirsty knew Iain was searching for her, even though he might not know it yet.

Kirsty had the advantage of knowing who he was. She recognised him from the day of his father's funeral eight months ago. He, being Iain Young, didn't even know Kirsty attended the funeral with her grandfather. He didn't know who her grandfather was, and so Iain knew nothing about her.

Kirsty's first instinct that day was to feel angry when Iain walked past them without speaking to her grandfather. He was so close they could have touched. Did he care so little about his father he didn't know that Joe was one of Drew's best and oldest friends?

Kirsty had to change her mind a few minutes later when she saw Iain's face. The expression was fleeting, but she had seen the desolation when Iain stared at the casket. She suspected he had an iron will and could control his emotions. He had pulled himself together. She could see how he buried his grief to help his younger siblings to deal with their pain.

For a moment, Kirsty had wondered who would take care of Iain. Her only consolation was that he wasn't alone in his grief. They were three siblings who could console each other.

When her grandfather passed away four months later, Kirsty didn't have that luxury. There was no family left for her to ease the burden.

Kirsty might not have a family, but she had her grandfather's loyal friends, the staff at Joe's and long-term customers. They helped her through her grieving.

Those were the times when she wished Drew was still alive. He had been her godfather and one of Joe's best friends.

Kirsty often wondered why they've never met Drew's family. She mentioned it to her grandfather once. She thought his friendship with her grandfather embarrassed Drew. Drew was a very wealthy and respected businessman.

It upset Joe that Kirsty could think that about his friend. He explained that Drew's wife, Cairsty, wasn't happy when Drew joined the army and went to fight in the Falklands war. For a while, she wanted nothing to do with Drew's army friends after he left the military. It had reminded her too much of the time she almost lost Drew.

Drew respected that. Cairsty had come around. She joined Drew when he was visiting Joe and his other army friends, but soon after, she became ill.

Joe had seen little of Drew while Cairsty was ill and after she passed away. Joe had still been in the army and stationed in Inverness. It didn't matter though. When Joe needed Drew a few months later when Kirsty's parents passed away, Drew was there for him.

When Kirsty arrived to live with her grandfather, Iain and his brother were at school. Drew worked long hours and sent the boys to live in the hostel at Merchiston. Drew planned his visits to Joe's when the children were away at school. According to Joe, Drew had guarded his time with them when they were at home.

Kirsty still had her doubts about it. To her, it was strange. How could none of the children have known of their father's involvement with Joe's?

That was also another anomaly. Drew bought the building about the time Kirsty's parents died, and she came to stay with Joe. Why did Drew keep it a secret from his children that he named a building after their mother? It was an answer she might never learn now.

Kirsty frowned when Iain's gaze drifted to her where she was standing behind the counter. For a moment, their eyes met and held. Kirsty held her breath until Iain broke eye contact and continued his perusal of the interior.

Kirsty took her time to study him. He had the same dark brown hair as Drew. He kept his cropped short and somehow messy on top as if he had pushed his hand through it several times. He also kept his beard and moustache cropped. The stubble did nothing to hide his full lower lip and the high cheekbones.

She didn't know much about men's fashion. She didn't have to. Kirsty would bet that Iain's outfit, from his designer suit and tie to the expensive Italian shoes, would cover her expenses for several months.

Her breath hitched when Iain's eyes returned to her. This time he was studying her for much longer. Kirsty couldn't look away from those blue eyes, her heart beating faster.

Iain broke eye contact first, and she could breathe again. He moved, taking slow yet measured steps to where Kirsty still stood with shaky legs.

He took a seat at the end of the counter and picked up the menu. He studied it with a frown, his eyes returning to her every few minutes.

Had he recognised her? Kirsty doubted that. There was no reason he should.

The other barista was busy, so Kirsty had no choice but to approach him to take his order. "Morning, have you decided on what kind of coffee you would like?"

Iain looked up from the menu and stayed quiet for so long Kirsty thought he didn't hear her. He frowned and said in a deep, gravelly voice that sent another ripple down her spine, "I don't drink coffee."

Kirsty almost gaped at him but pulled herself together before her chin hit the counter. She rolled her eyes and asked with veiled sarcasm, "You know that this is a coffee shop right? We have other drinks, but we primarily serve coffee."

He scowled at her, "I know. Unfortunately."

Unfortunately? Kirsty knew her earlier assumption about Iain was correct. He was trouble. She wished she could tell him to leave, but her grandfather's motto was never to be rude to her customers, even if you don't like them. They were their bread and butter. Her grandfather had then laughed and added. "And our coffee too".

Kirsty couldn't see Iain Young becoming one of her customers. She knew why he was here, but she wouldn't make it easy for him. She instead pretended she didn't know him.

Iain's sentences sounded clipped. His local Edinburgh burr was softer as if he spent some time away from the capital. Well, he had been. Kirsty knew that too. She heard many discussions between her grandfather and Drew Young over the years. Since Iain finished at Merchiston, he left the Scottish capital for Cambridge to complete his law studies.

Drew lamented that Iain didn't join the family business like his younger siblings. Drew's disappointment didn't matter. He was still proud of his eldest son. He told everyone willing to listen about Iain's legal career as a barrister in London. If Kirsty had to believe his father's proud boastings, he had been a good one too.

Kirsty ignored it and his surliness. "Do you want me to brew you a coffee or would you prefer tea or hot chocolate?"

"I'll try a coffee," he grunted.

Kirsty wanted to laugh. Judging by his mutinous face, coffee might be the last thing he wanted. She teased, "You know they say if you had one taste of this ambrosia, you'd be a converted soul?"

Iain snorted, "Don't be ridiculous."

Kirsty suppressed her smile when she turned away. Iain was reluctant to try the coffee, but for some or other reason he was forcing himself to do it. Turning her back to him, she tried to figure out what to give him. She always believed that the less you add to a good roast, the better. It might, however, not be the best choice for Iain.

A latte might be a better option, seeing he wasn't a regular coffee drinker. It consisted of creamy foam milk, and Iain could add as much espresso as he wished. It was also quick to prepare and easy to drink. She might get Iain out of Joe's before he scared away her customers with his surliness.

If Kirsty had to judge Iain's dark mood, she should give him two or three shots of espresso, but she stuck to one. She still had her pride and reputation. If she could convince him that coffee wasn't the drink of the devil, she might persuade him to keep Joe's.

No, struck that. She didn't need to convince Iain of anything. She had a valid contract, and he couldn't do anything about it.

She knew why Iain was here. Aileen and Graeme couldn't convince her to move, so Iain came to take care of business himself. What Iain Young didn't know, was that she would not give up Joe's. This was her home, her family and her past. Too many of her childhood memories were locked in this place. She couldn't give it up. If she did, it would feel as if she had failed her grandfather. She shook her head. That would not happen—not as long as she could help it.

She sighed and then concentrated on the task at hand. Kirsty started by frothing the milk to get the creamy texture she wanted. She then pulled a shot of espresso. The golden crema of the espresso still sat on top of the water when she finished. Kirsty breathed in the aroma. She would never tire of the rich smell of the coffee. It usually calmed her. Another of her grandfather's sayings sprung to mind, "Coffee was like a hug in a mug."

She served the espresso separately so Iain could add as much as he liked. Her eyes met Iain's when she slid the small tray with the latte in front of him. His eyes dropped to the black brew, the milky latte and studied it with trepidation. She sighed and explained the drink to her mutinous customer. "Coffee is an acquired taste. If you've tried before and you didn't like it, it might be because you haven't tried the right brew."

She ignored his frown and continued, "This is a latte. It is one of the simplest coffee drinks. It is your choice how much of the espresso you want to add."

Kirsty watched as Iain lifted the espresso to smell the aroma. He moved it away from his face, but then brought it back a second time for an even deeper sniff. His eyes closed as if he was enjoying the aroma. Kirsty watched fascinated as Iain opened his eyes again and studied the espresso in his hand. He added only a small amount to the milk then brought the mug to his lips to take a tentative sip. He rolled the liquid in his mouth, as he would've done when tasting a good whisky or wine. He then went back, added almost half the contents of the espresso to the mug, and took a second and third sip. He nodded and took another sip.

He put the mug on the counter and stared at it. Iain looked surprised as if he didn't expect to enjoy the experience. He looked up at Kirsty again, and this time she could even hear the surprise in his voice when he admitted, "It's good. Thank you."

Kirsty suppressed her smile and turned away to attend to other customers. When she finished, Iain was still sipping his latte while he studied the coffee shop with a frown. She could only hope that with his attitude, Iain would not stay too long.

When he put the mug down, Kirsty stopped in front of him asking, "Would you like anything else? Another cup of coffee or something to eat?"

He shook his head, his gaze sliding once more over the shop before he said, "I'm looking for a Miss Kirstine Brown. Is she here?"

She tried to ignore the uneasy feeling. Kirsty pulled the now empty mug away from in front of him before admitting, "I'm Kirstine Brown. What can I do for you?"

She noticed his surprise, as if she wasn't who or what he expected. He tried to hide it and held his hand out towards her, "Iain Young. I would like to speak to you. In private, please."

Kirsty signalled to Morag to take over. As she approached Iain, he stood up, but Kirsty didn't stop. He made her uneasy, so she didn't want to take him to her office. The space was too small to cope with Iain Young and his antagonism.

She also didn't want her patrons or the staff to overhear their conversation. Nothing might come of it, and she didn't want to upset them when it wasn't necessary.

Kirsty waited for customers to enter, greeting them and stepped outside. When she felt Iain's presence behind her, she turned to face him.

She didn't feel calm. Her heart was racing faster than a race-horse, but she would not let Iain see it. Being as smart a lawyer as Iain's father boasted, Kirsty might never get a word in if she let him get the upper hand. Her grandfather always said that attack was the best part of a defence. She hoped she sounded firm and calm when she told him, "Mr Young, I've made it clear to your minions I'm not interested in moving. I have a legal contract, which my lawyers assure me is non-negotiable. Stop harassing me."

"Miss Brown…" Iain started, but Kirsty stopped him, "I'm not interested. Goodbye."

She stepped around him and entered the coffee shop without a backward glance. She heard when the door shut behind her and holding her head up high, walked towards her office. She let out the breath she had been holding when she was alone in her office. Closing her eyes, she refused to let the tears that threatened slip out.

She had promised her grandfather to keep his legacy, and if it meant fighting her landlord, she would do it even if it was Drew Young's son.

She hadn't felt threatened by his brother or his sister. Not even that sleazy property manager who first came to see Kirsty had managed that.

Iain Young was different.

When she looked into his bright blue eyes and saw his firm stance, Kirsty didn't feel threatened. Not by his treats anyway.

No, she was more scared about the feelings he evoked.

2

I ain stared at the door after it closed behind Kirstine Brown. What did the hell happen?

He couldn't believe it. Did Kirsten Brown just throw him out of Joe's? Considering he was standing outside and she was inside, proved that she did. He shook his head in bewilderment.

He wasn't sure whether he should be angry with her or admire her for the cool, calm manner in which she did it. Admiration won hands down. Hell, he could now admit. He already admired her since he set foot in Joe's. He couldn't keep his eyes off her. And yes, he wanted to ask her on a date before he knew who she was.

The first time Iain's eyes had met Kirsty's he felt the rippling down his spine, a sure sign of his attraction. In that split second, he had taken in the honey-blonde hair she had tied in a plait hanging over one shoulder. The golden-brown eyes and sun-kissed skin gave her a healthy, vital look.

His eyes had lingered far too long on her full mouth and her slight frame when she preceded him to the door.

If it were different circumstances, he would like to get to know her better. Much better.

Even now he knew who she was Iain still felt tempted.

That was Iain's problem. He didn't have time for himself these days. That was why he wanted to get rid of this building. He had enough to worry about apart from a structure that needs more work than its worth.

Still shaking his head, Iain got into the waiting car. He wished he had the time to walk back to Tollcross via the Water of Leith Walkway. It was a few miles, but it might've helped to work off his frustration and clear his head. That was out of the question. An hour out of his schedule was something he couldn't afford these days.

Iain leaned his head back against the seat and breathed in deep. Usually, he would've worked as soon as he got in the car. Today he didn't have the energy to do that. It wasn't surprising. When last had he taken a break or did something for himself? He never switched off or relaxed anymore. The business occupied his mind even when he wasn't at the office.

David was watching him in the rear-view mirror. Iain could swear the older man was amused.

Iain pushed that ridiculous thought to the back of his mind. The visit to Leith hadn't been a complete disaster. It had one advantage, and that was reminding Iain that he needed to win back his life. Since his father's passing, Iain had done nothing but concentrate on business. It had been his choice, though. He had worked instead of dealing with losing his father, his career and his girlfriend at the same time. It was catching up with him now.

If he doesn't make a change soon, he and his siblings will burn out before long. As CEO, he could make that decision on his own, but Iain didn't operate like that. Young's was a family business. If they make a significant change in the company, he wanted his sister and brother to agree to it.

He pondered over it. Not that the company was in bad shape. It was quite the opposite. It's doing well, but the problem was that his father had fingers in too many pies. Remembering his parent, Iain knew his father liked the chase of a new acquisition. Over the last few years, he had acquired more and more properties and established businesses. Most of them were so diverse that it didn't even make sense. It wasn't as if his father concentrated on Scotland. No, some of those properties were in England, Ireland and also in France and Spain.

Properties, yes, that was also okay. Managing them was easy. It was the other businesses Drew bought that drove Iain nuts. What the hell did he know about a chocolate shop in Paris or a wine farm in Spain? Iain barely knew enough about the whisky distilleries his father acquired and hell, he's a Scot. He knew something about whisky. It was the diverse nature of the portfolio that made it difficult to manage them.

His mind drifted away from the business back to Joe's. Iain felt irritated. The company should be Iain's first and primary concern, but that wasn't what occupied his mind right now. That worried him. He should focus on the building and not the beautiful new owner of Joe's. He should remember what happened the last time he had been this interested in a woman. It had ended poorly then. With his track record, he wouldn't be surprised if the next relationship would end similarly. He knew what kind of man he was. He fell head over heels for a beautiful face, only to be disillusioned a few months later. By then, it was too late, and he was in too deep.

No, it wouldn't be worth it. Not again.

Iain sighed. Why did his father bequeath that building to him? It hadn't been part of Young's, although Young's managed the building and its tenants.

Since he learned of his inheritance, Iain had been in two minds about the building. If he could sell it, it would be one thing less needing his attention. The other option was to tear the old building down and redevelop it into a modern office block. That would be the most sensible solution.

Iain had thought a lot about it over the last month. Leith was getting a facelift so it wouldn't be a bad idea to hold on to the property. The longer he waited to decide, the more favourable the redevelopment sounded. Iain was getting excited about starting such a project. He had even mentioned it to his siblings.

Iain could follow neither recourse if he couldn't get rid of that one tenant and Kirstine Brown seemed obstinate.

He was no closer to a solution about the building than he had been when he set off earlier. The woman didn't even want to speak to him, but she didn't know Iain Young. He could be as tenacious as a terrier. Iain just needed to convince her to move to a different venue.

David took the fastest route via Holyrood and the Grassmarket, but it took half an hour longer. Building works at the upper end of Leith Road resulted in closed lanes. Traffic wasn't even peaking yet. It would be so much worse in two hours.

If he'd known it would take so long to reach the monstrosity of a building that housed Young's headquarters, he would've walked.

The extended trip had its advantages, though. Iain had enough time to think, excluding those about his frustrating tenant. He needed to get his life back. It would take careful planning and time. And the sooner he started, the better.

Still stuck in traffic, Iain took out his phone. He sent two texts before he changed his mind.

As soon as he reached the office, Iain called his brother and sister in for a meeting. Aileen and Graeme arrived together and picked up on Iain's frustration. They couldn't miss it, as Iain was pacing up and down with a scowl on his face. He saw the amusement on Graeme's face when he said, "So, I guess you also hadn't convinced the wee woman? Have you lost your charm, big brother?"

Iain scowled. He knew Graeme was teasing, but it didn't help. He glared at Graeme. "She didn't even give me a chance. She almost threw me out of Joe's. And you know what was the most frustrating? She did it so calmly and ladylike, I didn't even realise she did it! There I was, standing outside, and she was back inside with the door closing behind her!"

This time his brother and sister didn't even try to hide their amusement. They both burst out laughing. Aileen's eyes were sparkling when she asked, "So what do you think of Kirstine Brown? She's beautiful, isn't she?"

Kirstine's face flashed before his eyes, shocking Iain on how clearly he remembered the brown eyes and the honey-blonde hair. He felt the same ripple as he had earlier. He frowned and sat down behind his desk.

"It doesn't matter if she's beautiful or not. It doesn't solve my problem."

"Are you giving up on the project then?" Graeme asked, amused.

"I didn't say that. Miss Brown doesn't know me yet. I don't give up as easily as that. No, but I need to be prepared. I'm convinced that we need to get into Leith as soon as possible. Since I have the building, it would make sense to redevelop it. It's prime real estate. You said I have no legal foot to stand on?"

Graeme joined the legal department fresh out of law school. Since then he became head of the legal department. After their father's passing, Graeme became Vice-President of Operations. It meant he took over the day-to-day running of the company.

Graeme now sighed, "Bro', as a former practising barrister you're an even better lawyer than me. You went through the contract. I don't know why Dad added that. It makes little sense that you can't sell the building or tear it down while Joe's was still a tenant. Of all the rental agreements, it was only included in Joe's. Of all the tenants in the building, only Joe got an unlimited lease term. The others got two years or one-year contracts," Graeme pointed out.

Graeme frowned, "I don't understand it. I didn't draw up that contract, so it must have been Dad."

Iain sighed, "I know. What had Dad been thinking? What was it with Joe's?"

He played with his pen, tapping it on the desk while he was thinking.

"It would not help to speculate. I'll give it three months. If Miss Brown still doesn't want to move, I won't be able to do a thing. Aileen, I want you to look at other possibilities in Leith. I want in there as soon as possible before other developers get in. If Dad's instincts were right, which usually was, Leith would boom in the next few years. In the meantime, give the other tenants notice. I want the rest of that building empty. I may play dirty, but if there are no other tenants in the building, Miss Brown might bite."

"It isn't 'may play dirty', it is playing dirty, Iain. I've never known you to be so devious," Aileen said surprised.

Iain snorted, "Don't you know yet, Sis? I'm a lawyer. We're always devious."

Aileen shook her head, "No, I don't believe it but anyway, have you been in the building? When I went to see Miss Brown, I inspected it. It's so beautiful. It has the same architectural style as the old police office and railway station in Leith which, as you know, are A-listed buildings. It needs work, like cleaning the outside and painting inside. You may need to touch up the woodwork, but I still feel it would be a shame to tear it down."

Iain shook his head. He had focused on convincing the obstinate Miss Brown to move and never even looked at the building. Maybe he should've been more observant. Aileen rarely gets misty-eyed over buildings, but perhaps she had a point. Before he could ask her, Aileen's gaze shifted between her two brothers.

"Have neither of you noticed the name of the building?"

Both Iain and Graeme shook their heads confused. Aileen looked close to crying when she said, "The building's name is Cairistìne Court."

They all sat there, quiet for a while, remembering their mother who died when Aileen was only six years old. Aileen mused, "Do you think it is a coincidence?"

"What?" Iain frowned, so Aileen explained, "Cairistìne Court? Kirstine Brown? I know it has a different spelling, but I wonder. It could be a sign."

Both men groaned. "No, don't even start," Iain stopped his sister. "I don't have time for that now. I want a solution, not more complications."

He frowned, "I don't understand why Dad never mentioned Cairistìne Court or Joe's. Why had we never heard of a building which might bear Mum's name or Dad's friendship with Joe and Kirstine? If I have to look at the registration documents, he bought that building after Mum died. Joe was one of his first tenants."

He shook his head, "I can't find any records, but it's no use wondering about it now. Anyway, I want to discuss something else with you and would like to know what you think."

Both his siblings sobered up when they realised that Iain was serious. They nodded and waited for him to explain.

"Adapting without Dad for the last eight months had been difficult for all three of us. I couldn't have done it without you, taking over the business like this. I wanted to thank you for doing it with me. I didn't think I would like to be a businessman when I took over, but I'm enjoying it."

The other two laughed. Both remembered Iain's stubbornness in joining Young's after law school.

He smiled too, but then he sobered up again. "This is a difficult decision, and as Young's belongs to the family, it concerns all three of us."

Iain sighed, "Driving back from Leith made me realise something. It was sobering to tell you the truth. You will both agree with me that we haven't had time for ourselves running the company for the last six or seven months. I have done nothing for myself during that time, apart from our weekly squash games. When last has anyone of us had a break, even for a weekend? When we get together, we talk about business. I don't want to live like this for the rest of my life. I don't want to die on the job like Dad."

Graeme chuckled, "Yeah, I can't remember when last I've been on a date, and neither have you two. Man, I need to get laid. Soon."

Aileen put her hands over her ears, "Too much information, Big Brother. I don't want to hear about your sex life."

Graeme snorted, "What sex life? It's non-existent."

"I still don't want to hear about your sex life or the lack thereof," Aileen argued. "Would you like it when I tell you about mine?"

Both brothers frowned. Iain scowled at Aileen, "I don't want to know. If I catch one man even looking at you, I'll kill him."

Aileen snorted, "Come on, Brother. It's too late for that. For goodness sake, I'm twenty-seven, not eighteen! I'll date whoever I want to."

Both brothers folded their arms. Graeme grunted, "They have to get past us first."

Aileen shook her head, "Rather worry about your own love life and leave mine alone. Anyway, you moan about your time. If we don't talk about business now, it'll be another late night. What do you still want to discuss?"

Iain frowned at her, but he explained, "I had time to study the assets of the company. I didn't realise that Dad had bought so many new businesses. We need to decide. It's good to have diversity in the company, but not as much as we have. Do you agree, Aileen?"

Iain directed his question to his sister as she knew the portfolio the best. Aileen had studied property management and joined the company after university.

"Yes," Aileen agreed. "I spoke to Dad about it, but he was reluctant to sell anything."

Iain pursed his lips, "I know the company is doing well, but we need to think about streamlining it. I would like you both to come up with ideas on how to do it. I'll do the same. We can discuss it in a week or two."

Aileen looked excited at the prospect. She would start with her analysis tonight if he didn't stop her. That was why he wanted to bring up the other point again. "We need to make sure we have time away from the business, starting now.

Spend time with your friends. Go away or do something, please. I promise I'll do the same."

Aileen bit her lip, "Can I have first dibs for a weekend away?" she asked.

Both brothers turned to her and asked, "You have a date?"

Aileen flushed, but she looked at her brothers, "No, I don't have a date, but Elizabeth Johnston is getting married. I would like to go. The wedding is in three weeks, close to Inverness."

Iain and Graeme looked at each other and then Iain shrugged, "Fine with me. I have no definite plans yet."

"Me neither, but I'll let you know. The boys had nagged for a while now that we should go hiking in Skye. What about you, Iain?"

"I have nothing specific yet, but when something comes up, I may take the opportunity. It would be nice to hang out with my friends. I would like to suggest something in the meantime."

"What is it?" Aileen and Graeme asked at the same time.

Iain grinned, "You know that pub in South Queensferry we used to go to with Dad? They used to have a nice Sunday lunch special."

The other two nodded. Iain explained, "Why don't we go there for lunch on Sunday, and we make it a rule we don't talk about the business?"

"That would already be a nice break. If we are at home, we always end up in the study talking business. If we aren't at the house, we may even relax," Aileen agreed.

Iain stood up as a sign that the meeting was over. He picked up the stack of documents from his desk and walked to the door to hand it to his secretary. He turned back to his siblings, who had followed him. "Okay, that's it then, and since it is Friday, I will finish early today and do what my friends do."

"And what's that?" Graeme asked. "Read a book?"

Iain snorted, "I'm not so boring. I go out."

He trailed off, realising what he was saying and then clarified, "Okay, rarely, but I go out sometimes. Tonight, I'm going out with Duncan and Rab."

This time Graeme snorted, "Those two? They're worse than you are, Bro'. All you will do is discuss the merits of staying in the EU or something like that. I can imagine how exciting that must be."

Iain swiped one hand and hit Graeme on the head. It resulted in Graeme grabbing Iain around the neck. When they wrestled with each other, he heard Aileen sigh. Moira's stern voice interrupted them, "Boys, how many times have I told you not to play inside. Take it outside—preferably where the rest of the staff can't see you."

Both Iain and Graeme stopped what they were doing. With their arms still around each other, they apologised, "Yes, Ma'am. Sorry, Ma'am."

They then looked at each other and burst out laughing.

Moira had been his father's secretary when their father was still a judge. When he took over the business, Moira came with him. She had been part of their lives as long as they could remember. When Iain looked back at her, he noticed her loving smile and knew that she had missed their antics too. It had been a long time since they had laughed like this and proved to Iain that he was right. They needed their lives back.

Once in the car, Iain leaned back against the seat. His mind drifted back to the conversation he had with his siblings. Graeme hit the nail on the head. Iain, like Graeme, hadn't dated in the months since Iain's return to Edinburgh. Being with a woman wasn't even a consideration. His sex life was non-existent. He wasn't a social recluse. Iain, like his siblings, still belonged to Edinburgh's social scene, but that was it. Most nights, when Iain attended a function, he was so tired or didn't enjoy it. He always kept in mind that he still had a briefcase full of paperwork to go through before he could go to sleep.

He was lonely. It was as simple as that.

Iain's association with one of his fellow lawyers in London ended when he returned to his home country. Lydia was far too ambitious and couldn't understand how Iain could come home and run his father's company. He wondered what Lydia would have done if she knew how much the company was worth. He was cynical enough to know that if she had, she would've changed her mind. Lydia would have had no qualms to further their relationship to her advantage.

Iain only felt relief when their relationship had ended. He'd known long before then that the relationship had run its course.

He wasn't the first one in his family who had to choose to end his legal career. His father had already been a judge when he had to give up his career. Iain's uncle Rory had run the company then. He had neither wife nor an heir, so his father had no choice. Iain still thought his father's heart wasn't in the business. He had good instincts, though, and it worked most of the time.

His mind flitted again to Kirstine Brown. She was the first woman in eight months who interested him enough even to consider dating. He had met many beautiful women during this time, especially the Edinburgh socialites. None of them had affected him as Kirstine had. Why? What was it about her?

Iain only needed to close his eyes to know why. Kirstine was beautiful, even without visible makeup and fancy clothes. Her skin looked so soft and flawless that Iain had itched to stroke his finger over her cheek. He wanted to untie her hair and drag his fingers through it, tasting those full lips...

Hell, he couldn't think about that. He made a vow when he took over the company. He would not mix business with pleasure, as that was only looking for trouble.

He had one choice, though, and that was to change his attitude. It may make Kirstine Brown more malleable. He grinned.

He might even enjoy it.

3

It was a chilly and *dreich* day, even for the middle of April, and supposed to be springtime. The temperatures had dropped to freezing point. It felt much worse because of the warmer and sunny weather in the last few days. Yesterday the day temperatures were close to double figures. This was Edinburgh though. It wasn't unusual for this time of year.

It was warm and cosy inside Joe's, and the pre-work crowd filled the place. There were only a few seats available at the counter, and the queue for takeaway had grown in the last half an hour.

Kirsty didn't always look up when the door to the coffee shop opened, but this time she did. She groaned.

She knew Iain would come back, but she wasn't ready for him yet. Their previous encounter and the effect he had on her was still too fresh.

She needed to be strong, though. If Iain thought she would be pleasant to him today, he was in for a big surprise. She didn't have time to chitchat, and anyway, he would be the last person she wanted to speak to right now. Kirsty sighed when he walked over, his gaze sliding over her while he approached. The blue eyes were as penetrating as she remembered from their previous encounter.

It had the same effect on her as it had then.

Iain slid into the seat opposite her, so close that Kirsty could see the raindrops still clinging to his hair. He shrugged out of his coat and hung it over the chair behind him, and then he looked at her—watching her without saying a word. That was even more unnerving than his previous surly behaviour.

Kirsty knew she was rude, but this man could unnerve her, and she couldn't afford it to happen. Particularly not with him. She glared at him and asked, "What do you want?"

Unlike the last time he had been here, Iain didn't glare at her. This time his mouth curled up, and his eyes twinkled when he asked with almost the same sarcasm Kirsty had the previous Friday, "I thought this is a coffee shop. You make coffee?"

Kirsty scowled at him. She could feel her heart beating fast, and her legs felt like jelly when he smiled. That smile was devastating.

"*Aye*, so it is, but don't expect to get it on the house again. What would you like?" she grumbled.

His eyes widened when he realised what Kirsty implied. A flush crept up his cheekbones, even visible through his beard. He looked at a loss for words, which might be the first for a glib lawyer like him and only mumbled, "I'm sorry. I didn't mean to... What do I owe you?"

For a fleeting moment, Kirsty felt sorry for him, but she squashed that thought as quickly as it surfaced. She lifted her chin as she surveyed him, careful not to look into his eyes. Combined with his smile, that would be her downfall.

Kirsty might've sounded a wee bit smug when she said, "Nothing."

She kept her face as stoic as possible and demanded, "What would you like today?"

"Surprise me," Iain replied.

Kirsty rolled her eyes. "That's not helping much but let me see what I can do. Do you like milk, cream or foam? Do you like nuts or vanilla or...?"

"All of them," he replied with another grin. Kirsty turned her back on him, rolling her eyes again. Geez, what was it with this man? She would have preferred the grumpy and rude man from the previous week. Today he was far too friendly and attractive, but Kirsty didn't trust him. Her grandfather had always quoted a famous writer who said you should not trust a man who didn't drink coffee. She should do well to remember that—especially with Iain Young.

Today the light blue shirt and navy suit accentuated Iain's eyes. She almost snorted. As if he needed that. It was not fair that such a jerk should have such beautiful eyes. In Kirsty's opinion, it was a complete waste—and it was unfair.

Several other women in the coffee shop had also noticed Iain and sent furtive glances his way. Kirsty felt irritated with the women's undeniable attraction to him. It didn't matter whether she agreed with their assessment. He still made her hackles rise. Her irritation shifted to Iain. He seemed oblivious to the women. It might be because he kept his eyes on her. It irritated Kirsty. She shouldn't have noticed the women's reaction nor Iain's perusal.

The women's attention brought an unnecessary emotion—jealousy. It was stupid. She shouldn't let Iain Young affect her so much.

Another of Joe's wisdom popped up in her head. Never brew a coffee in a temper as your thoughts and emotions go into the brew.

Kirsty calmed her thoughts, albeit reluctantly. If she had a choice, she would rather have given Iain cramps. He might then stay away and stop bugging her. She shifted her thoughts to her grandfather.

Her grandfather had been a widower when he took her in when she was six. Joe put aside his grief when he lost his only son and his daughter-in-law in South Africa because of a car accident. He gave up his military career to take care of his only granddaughter. Through their grief, they had built a bond in those first months after Kirsty arrived from South Africa. It all happened right here in the coffee shop Joe had opened after her arrival. He had been her rock from the moment he brought her home, through her teenage years, until he died. He still was. He and Joe's was Kirsty's whole life.

She went to university on Joe's insistence but did nothing with her business degree, other than managing Joe's. She didn't need a degree to run Joe's. Her grandfather taught her the most important lessons she needed.

Glancing back at Iain, she noticed that he was still studying her. While the espresso had brewed, she had textured the milk. Her hand shook, and Kirsty had to take a deep breath before she could layer a cappuccino. She used the spoon to hold back the foam and filled the cup with about one-third full of steamed milk. She added the espresso, then spooned frothed milk on top.

Kirsty debated which art to use. No way was she going for the quickest option of the heart today but not for Iain. A thistle could've worked, but that kind of latte art was a skill practised by well-trained and practised baristas. Designs like that were intricate and took time. Today she didn't have the time and opted for a leaf.

She put the large cup in front of him, without looking at him. His eyes were still too unnerving to do that. She murmured, "Cappuccino with foam," and turned away before she made a fool of herself.

To avoid Iain, Kirsty went on her rounds through the shop. She chatted with her regulars. She didn't have to look to know that Iain was still watching her as she could feel his eyes burning into her back.

His lips curled into a smile when he left. When the door closed behind Iain, Kirsty exhaled with relief, eliciting a sly smile from Morag.

Without even realising that she was doing it, Kirsty's eyes followed Iain through the window. There was a car waiting at the curb, but Iain didn't get in. He turned and gazed up, studying the four-storey building for a long time. He lowered his head, and then he looked at the coffee shop again. Before Kirsty could duck away, Iain smiled and lifted his hand in a wave, before he turned and got in the car. Kirsty felt as if she could die of embarrassment.

Iain had known she had been watching him. He had not been the only one, Kirsty realised, as Morag came to stand by her and said, "So, do you have a new admirer?"

Kirsty scowled, "Not on your life! That was Drew's eldest."

Morag gaped at her, "Are you serious? Tsk, Drew never let on that his son was so attractive. Maybe you should've let them arrange that blind date for you he and your grandfather nagged about?"

Kirsty snorted, "Those two? No, do you think I could trust them after Lachlan?"

Morag scowled, "Yeah, that was not one of their best matchmaking efforts."

Kirsty nodded, "Lachlan did enough to put me off those smooth city boys."

"So, is the eldest Young... that sounds weird, doesn't it? But anyway, is he going to follow in his father's footsteps and frequent Joe's?"

Kirsty scowled and shook her head, "No, all Iain Young is interested in is to get me to close Joe's or move to another building. I don't know what he wants to do with the building, but if he thinks I'll sit back and let him tear it down, he's in for a big surprise. I can't let him do that. Not only for Joe but for his father too."

Morag nodded. Kirsty didn't have to explain. Drew had been very sentimental about this building that carried his late wife's name. He would turn in his grave if Iain tore it down.

Kirsty would not give him that chance.

IAIN SCOWLED at the email in front of him. Damn, he thought he would've made progress so far, but Kirstine Brown was more stubborn than he was.

Tried as he might, he couldn't get closer to her.

He tried to reason. No success. He tried arguments. Still nothing. He used charm. Nope, nothing. Zilch. Zero. What else could he do to get her to talk to him? He went to Joe's every Monday, Wednesday and Friday but he made no progress. She refused to speak to him.

He tried emailing her. At first, her answer came back with only one word. *No*. His weekly emails increased to daily ones, but still nothing. Although her answers were longer than the first week's, her response always stayed no.

It was as if they were sparring with each other. Iain had to admit that he was looking forward to opening his email in the morning. Hell, he even smiled twice at her haughty replies. She would throw back his arguments in his face, and he liked it. No, she was not stupid, and she knew what she was talking about. It intrigued him, more than was healthy.

Iain caved in and called Dougie Munroe, Kirstine's lawyer. Dougie hadn't wasted time. They exchanged pleasantries as Iain would with any of his father's friends.

When Iain had mentioned Cairistìne Court and Joe's, Dougie was first reluctant to discuss it. He had no choice, though. As the lawyer for Joe's, Dougie had to. His first words of advice to Iain were that he would waste his time in trying to get Joe's out of the building. The contract was valid, and Iain could do nothing about it.

Iain could hear the resignation in the lawyer's voice when he said, "Let me tell you something, Iain. I'm Joe's lawyer. Your father had approached me to represent Joe's. When he and Joe arrived here with the contract, I had advised your father about its ridiculousness. I refused their choice to sign it on the first day they were here. I took the contract to several other lawyers and two judges. They all said the same. The deal is valid, and you would struggle to contest it in court. When they came back the next week to sign it, I had again advised against it, but I couldn't change their minds. They were adamant, so I had no choice. I let them sign it in front of two other lawyers in my firm, so I had witnesses to prove that I advised them against it. They signed, of course. They were two stubborn men."

Dougie cleared his throat and added, "I looked at the contract again after Joe's death. It specifies that it was with Joe's Coffee House—not Joe in his personal capacity. Whoever the owner of Joe's was, had the right to keep Joe's where it was. Kirstine is the only one who can now decide if she wanted to close Joe's doors or move to another location. She had to do it out of her own free will, Iain. You can't force Joe's out if the owner does not want to move and my advice to you would be to leave Kirstine alone. Do not speak to her again about the matter without me being present."

Iain sighed, "Had my father been out of his mind?"

Dougie chuckled, "Your father and Joe were both sane. They had the papers to prove it and anyway, they signed that last contract two years before your father's death."

Dougie's final words before he rang off made Iain more confused than he'd been before this discussion. The older man had said to Iain, "Your father had a reason for doing it. You should try to find out what it was."

"How?" Iain had asked, frustrated.

Dougie chuckled, "Your answer is in Joe's."

Before Iain could answer, the line went dead.

Iain pondered over his discussion with Dougie, so he went back to Joe's. More than once.

Why was it such a big deal for Kirstine to move Joe's? A coffee shop could do business anywhere. Joe's could move to another part of Edinburgh where it would make a much larger profit.

Kirstine looked upset with him every time he walked in. Iain hated it. The weeks turned into months, but Iain still didn't find his answer. How could he find it if Kirstine didn't speak to him? Every time he was there, he attempted to rattle her by being his most charming, but she didn't bite. It grated on him that she didn't like him. He understood why, but there was nothing he could do about it. Other than taking his order, Kirstine ignored him. Sometimes she went so far by disappearing into her office. It didn't matter. Iain was convinced, as Dougie had pointed out, that he would find his answer in Joe's. He needed patience.

Getting his life back wasn't as easy as Iain had thought it would be. He made a point of going home earlier at least two or three times a week. In the evenings Iain made it back before dark, he went for a jog on the beach. He went out with his friends. He even dated during the first month. Often, in fact. He didn't enjoy it and gave up trying.

He attended the business receptions and the Edinburgh social scene when necessary. Iain still didn't like the stuffy dinners favoured by the Edinburgh elite. He had enough of those when he lived in London. His friends had to drag Iain to go with them to some of those functions. That also didn't happen often. Rab was away most of the time with Doctors without Borders, and Duncan had his head in his books.

It was discomforting that the highlight of Iain's life was his visits to Joe's. He dared not reflect on it yet, but he would need to do it soon.

Graeme and Aileen had also attempted to spend less time on business and more on their social lives. All three of them agreed that it had felt good to do so. Nothing would change before Iain did something with the company and his other assets. Cairistine Court caused Iain more headaches than anything else did.

Five weeks after his discussion with Dougie, Iain didn't need an excuse to get Joe's out of the building anymore. Aileen had found the properties in Leith Iain requested and in the previous week, they had closed on both. One building had been empty. The team of renovators would start with the renovations next month. The second property was a rare empty plot close to the water where Iain planned an office park and entertainment areas. They would meet with the architects and planning committees in the following weeks.

The siblings analysed Young's portfolio and streamlining Young's management. Both Aileen's and Graeme's reports confirmed Iain's initial findings. Since he received their feedback, he had been busy, and today it was crunch time. They needed to decide.

Early that morning, he had sent them messages to meet him at the office before they did anything else that day. Iain had David stopping at Joe's getting takeaway coffee, something the older man didn't find strange. David's remark one morning reminded Iain of the expression he'd seen on David's face that first time he went to Joe's. He hadn't been wrong then. David said it felt weird to drive to Joe's again a few times a week. Iain then knew his father had done it too. It still puzzled him. Iain was on the brink of asking David about it when they arrived at the office.

His siblings and Moira looked surprised when he walked into the office with four cups with Joe's written on it. They all knew he'd never drank coffee. Iain ignored their curiosity and handed them each a cup. Nobody, apart from David, knew about Iain's visits to Joe's—or so he thought.

Iain would not give them a chance to speculate. He sat down, opened his cup and breathed in the aroma. He sighed and took his first appreciative sip before he put his cup down.

Opening his briefcase, he took out the folders he had taken home last night. Only then did he look up and notice his siblings' amused faces. Iain ignored them. This wouldn't be the time to discuss his fascination with Joe's.

No, if Iain wanted to tell the truth, it would be to Joe's lovely owner.

When Moira left, Iain looked down at the two documents in front of him. "I went through your reports about stream-lining the business. We all agree that we need to do something. I put out feelers in the last week. I got two offers yesterday, both from the same investment group. The one offer is for the whole company. The second offer is for our residential portfolio, including the new developments."

Iain slid one document over the desk for his siblings to read. They leaned together to read the first page and then both looked up, shocked. Graeme was the first to get his voice back. "Over two hundred and fifty million pounds for the residential portfolio! Are you serious?"

Iain nodded "Aye, and the offer for the whole company is for almost one billion pounds. I know the housing market is booming, but so is the commercial market. I made copies of the two offers for each of you. Why don't you take your time studying it, then we can meet tomorrow to decide?"

Both of his siblings still looked shocked when they stood up, each taking the folder Iain held out to them. They were quiet when they were leaving his office. He guessed they were trying to assimilate the information Iain had dumped on them. He didn't doubt that the news hadn't yet penetrated. When Iain received the offers, it shocked him. He only just managed to keep the poker face he had perfected for when he had appeared in Court.

The following day Iain and his siblings had discussed the offers at hand. As Iain suspected, they agreed to take the offer for the residential portfolio. The rest of the day, they considered what to do with the pending profit. When they went home that evening, they had agreed that fifty percent of the profit would go back into Young's. They would invest ten percent in a Trust fund to benefit various charities.

They would split a further ten percent amongst their staff as a bonus, which they will calculate it according to the number of years the employees had worked at Young's. The final thirty percent they would divide amongst them.

Two days later, they signed the contracts with the investment company in Glasgow. There was still a process and protocol to follow, but they had taken the first steps. On the way back from Glasgow they agreed that it was a relief.

The consensus was that Young's would make no further investments for the rest of the year. They had the two new acquisitions in Leith. They would concentrate on that for the coming year.

They had enough to consider. It was not only about business developments but also their personal lives. They grew up with having money. They attended private schools and had university degrees, but all three of them had worked for their salaries as their father stipulated. Now they were millionaires, and it was a lot to take in.

The staff at Young's had taken the announcement in their stride. The unexpected bonus might've softened the blow for those who would leave Young's to work for the new firm. Iain could rely on Graeme to negotiate who should remain at Young's and who should transfer.

Iain visited the properties remaining in their portfolio. While he had been away, he frequented other coffee shops, but somehow it didn't feel the same. After his return to Edinburgh the following week, Iain went back to Joe's. When he had walked into Joe's cosy interior, it almost felt like déjà vu, and it had shocked him how much he had missed it. To Iain, it felt like coming home, and it scared the hell out of him. Why was that, he wondered?

Now, in Joe's, he didn't have to wonder anymore.

Joe's had a certain charm that most of the other shops didn't have. The décor was warm, with wooden tables and chairs. In front of the fireplace was a leather couch with a large coffee table. In front of the dark wood counter was a row of bar chairs where Iain preferred to sit. Framed portraits covered one wall, books and old coffee pots filled the shelves.

Iain looked up and found Kirstine watching him. His heart slowed down. It had been a while since he'd seen her. He'd never stopped thinking about her while he was away. He could recall every single detail of her eyes, the golden flecks in her hair, the long, slender fingers... Hell, he could go on and on, because it felt as if Kirstine Brown was forever etched in his mind.

At first, he thought he only missed Joe's and the smell of the brewed coffee associated with Joe's.

Iain swallowed when the truth hit him.

He thought she was beautiful? No, she was far more than that.

4

Iain had to admit on Friday evening that the attraction he felt that first day he'd seen Kirstine and tried to ignore, was still there. Not that it helped him much if he had to judge by Kirstine's attitude.

He joined Rab and a few of his friends at the pub down the road from Joe's. It had become a familiar routine in the last few weeks if they didn't have another function or party or when Rab was in town. This was, however, the first time they went to this pub in Leith.

When he walked in with Rab after eight, the place was buzzing. One of Rab's friends waved them over to a table in the corner. Iain had accepted the introductions and had taken his seat and looked up when he heard a woman laugh close by. The sound had caused the same ripple effect he had felt the first day he had seen Kirstine. Iain had recognised it that day as a sign of attraction. It would be the same now. He could only hope that whoever this woman was would have the same effect face to face.

Without making it too obvious, he turned toward where he heard the laughter coming from. He drew a deep breath when he recognised the woman. He should've known. He felt it when he walked into Joe's and saw her on Wednesday. He was more attracted to this woman than he'd been to any other in a long time. So yes, he could understand his rapid heartbeat when he saw her. What he hadn't expected to feel, was the sudden flare of jealousy when he saw her in the company of a man. They looked like they knew each other well as they spoke and laughed.

She looked different tonight dressed in jeans and a light green sweater. Her hair was hanging over her shoulders. Iain couldn't keep his eyes off her, much to the disappointment of the single women at their table.

Seeing her, here was unexpected. Okay, seeing her outside of Joe's was surprising. He hadn't thought about it before, because he dared not think about Kirstine in a personal capacity. It was safer to keep her in Joe's, but now she had escaped that little cocoon in which he had held her.

One of the other men at their table exclaimed, "Hey, there's my favourite barista."

Again, the flare of jealousy hit Iain, and he frowned at the man who explained to his companion "She runs Joe's Coffee House."

The woman beamed. "Ooh, that's the place down the road with the nice cappuccinos. They also make the most delicious sandwiches."

"Yes, but it's not just the coffee, food and the atmosphere that makes Joe's such a nice place," Rab added. "Do you know that the employees don't take the tips? They use those jars with the money to give coffee and something to eat to war veterans who can't afford it."

The conversation around the table now focuses on Joe's. One man frowned, "I heard rumours that Joe's will close. The tenants in the building got a notice that the owner would not renew their contracts. I hope the owner of the building, whoever he is, knows what he's doing."

"I hope that's not true," one of the other's exclaimed. "I think we must hold a protest. Joe's can't close. It's an institution. I went there for my first grown-up date."

Iain inhaled, trying to bite back nausea. With everything that went on with the sale of their residential portfolio, Iain had forgotten about his instructions to give the tenants in Cairistìne Court notice.

Iain excused himself and went to the bathroom. He needed to escape the conversation around the table and the subsequent guilt.

He should have stopped the eviction of the tenants, but now it was too late. No wonder Kirstine didn't want to talk to him.

Deep in thought, he left the bathroom and walked straight into Kirstine. Her eyes widened when she recognised Iain. She stepped back as if she wanted to escape his touch. Iain dropped his hands which had lifted to hold her arms. She had been so close he could smell the slight vanilla fragrance that surrounded her. His voice sounded husky in his ears when he whispered her name.

"Kirstine..."

It felt strange hearing her name from his lips, but it felt good. He wanted to try it again, but Kirstine didn't give him a chance. She sounded sarcastic when she said, "Mr Young. I'm surprised to see you here. Are this pub and the neighbourhood not too common for you?"

Iain felt the anger flush through him. It was unexpected. How dare she judge him like that? She didn't know him. He frowned and wanted to reply, but Kirstine didn't give him a chance. She stepped around him and entered the bathroom.

Iain balled his hands in frustration. Why did the woman always leave him stranded and frustrated on the other side of the door? Hell, he usually wasn't as tongue-tied as this, but she made him look like a blubbering fool.

Iain had had enough. He called a cab and told Rab he was leaving while shrugging on his leather jacket. Iain ignored the protests. He sent one more glare in the direction of Kirstine's table and left. Outside he breathed in the salty sea air while he waited for the cab.

He was angry. Yes, mad at himself because he lost focus. He was so sidetracked by Kirstine Brown, baiting her that he forgot to focus on his business.

More so, he was angry about her unfair accusations. Was that how she saw him? A conceited snob that wouldn't socialise with people that had less than him? She didn't know him.

Well, if that was how she saw him, he needed to change her opinion of him and show her the person he was.

Hah! That resolution lasted as long as his anger. As soon as it dissipated, Iain knew that it was his pride and disappointment, which caused him to react like that. It would be far better to stay away from her if she had such a low opinion of him.

JUST WHEN SHE thought he had given up, this happened. She stared at Mr Douglas in dismay. The old lawyer nodded, "Yes, we've tried to negotiate, but no, we don't have a choice. Our contract is up in a month, and we'll be moving into a new building a few blocks away.

What was she going to do? Did he think if the building were empty, she would move too? Well, he was in for a big surprise. His building could stand empty for all she cared. She would stay here. She would fight for something in which Drew and Joe believed so strongly.

Before their encounter in Baird's the previous Friday, she almost liked him. Now she didn't. Morag had teased her about his regular visits and their emails since he came to Joe's on an almost daily basis. Not that they spoke much. Their only exchange was when she asked him what his order was and his reply was "Surprise me."

He challenged her, trying to find a new brew for him every time or making variations on his previous choices. He had gone through her whole range of warm blends, and now, since the weather became warmer as summer approached, he even tried the cold drinks.

She hated that she got to know his tastes. He liked cream and not sugar. He loved hazelnut and not chocolate, and so on. Kirsty could argue that she also identified some of her other customer's tastes, but she didn't want to know Iain's.

When she turned away from Mr Douglas, Morag was watching her. Kirsty shook her head and said, "Call a staff meeting for closing time."

Morag nodded. Kirsty found the safety of her office. She didn't want to speak to her staff yet. They might also have heard the rumours, and she had to reassure them. She didn't want to do that when she was angry or upset, and at that moment she was furious.

She might've underestimated him. He was more devious than she expected. Hell, he almost fooled her these last few months. He would not do it again. She pulled the phone closer and called her lawyer.

The short discussion with Dougie Munroe brought no more answers to what Iain was planning to do with the building. It reassured her that he couldn't do anything about her agreement.

She wasn't stupid, though. A significant percentage of their regular clientele came from this building. If their new premises was a short distance away, they might find a closer alternative than Joe's. Unless she could keep them coming to Joe's by providing a service. She knew most of them well. She knew their tastes and preferences. Not all of them came and sat down to have their coffee and sandwiches. Many of them had takeaways.

For the rest of the afternoon Kirsty made plans, thanking Joe for that business degree he insisted on her doing. When she met with her staff later that afternoon, she could reassure them that it didn't matter if the building above was empty. Joe's was staying where it was.

The employees and regular customers who had also heard the rumours were all relieved. Their loyalty helped Kirsty over the next few days.

IAIN'S RESOLUTION TO stay away from Joe's lasted a week. By Friday afternoon he had withdrawal symptoms, snapping at everyone who opposed him.

Even annihilating Graeme in their weekly squash game on Saturday didn't help. When they walked back to the changing rooms, Graeme asked with a smug smile, "So are you going to tell me what's biting you in the arse this week?"

Iain scowled but didn't reply. By the end of his shower, he knew what the answer was. He missed his caffeine fix, and he missed Joe's. And he missed a particular golden-eyed barista more than was healthy. So what the hell was he going to do about it?

He was going to Joe's. As Dougie said, his answer to that confusing contract still lies in Joe's. If he weren't there, he wouldn't find it.

When Iain told Graeme that they were going to Joe's for breakfast instead of having it at the Club, Graeme complained. Iain was adamant. Now he had decided to go back to Joe's, he didn't want to wait until Monday.

When he walked into Joe's, Iain felt the warm familiarity of the place envelop him. Iain got his answer as soon as he entered Joe's. He would not close Joe's. And the reason was not his desperate need for the caffeine he came to like or the frustrating contract. It was Joe's owner.

Iain could tell from a mile away that he had pissed her off. He had an idea why. Aileen had confirmed yesterday that the last tenants would move to their new premises in a few months. Iain had painted himself into a corner by giving the other tenants notice, but he didn't know how to fix that.

Iain barely knew Graeme flirted with some women part of the breakfast crowd in Joe's. It didn't even register that a couple of the women tried to flirt with him too. When one woman dropped a serviette in front of him with her phone number, Iain picked it up. As he did, he looked up, into Kirstine's eyes, and he knew it would not happen. No, hell, one glimpse in those expressive eyes and Iain had his answer.

It was more shocking and unexpected than Iain had anticipated. He was smitten. Utterly and firmly with the woman who held his eyes.

He crumbled the serviette and discarded it in his dirty plate.

Graeme gaped at him in surprise, but he stopped speaking when he realised Iain anyway hadn't even heard a word he was saying. Iain also missed his brother's amused expression flitting between him and Kirstine.

His heart beat loudly in his ears. He wouldn't have noticed if a bomb exploded next to him.

His brain went into overdrive, trying to figure out what he had to do. He had his work cut out for him to convince Kirstine to give him a chance. He didn't have to be a genius to know that. He would not have an easy task approaching her because she might doubt his intentions, and hell, he wouldn't blame her. He didn't have a good track record with her.

.   .   .

HIS ABSENCE in the past week had lulled her into complacency. He had never been to Joe's over a weekend, and Kirsty hadn't expected to see him on Saturday morning. It had been a surprise and a shock. She didn't even want to think about the thrill she experienced, the sudden exhilaration of her heartbeat when their eyes met.

She might contribute the faster heartrate with the way he looked today. Geez, she thought he looked good in a suit. Nope, he looked even better in black jeans and a blue Henley shirt that stretched tight over his chest and arms. He had combined that with a black leather jacket which he took off when he entered with his brother.

Kirsty swallowed the drool and busied herself by cleaning the countertop for the umpteenth time. That was until Morag grabbed the cloth from her hand. Kirsty looked at her, surprised, "What did you do that for?"

Morag smirked, "Instead of cleaning the counter, wipe your drool."

Kirsty scowled, but she didn't argue. Her gaze slid back to where the two brothers now made their way to the counter. She groaned. Hell, one Young brother was enough. Two of them? No wonder all the women in Joe's sat up straight.

Where it looked like Iain didn't notice the women's flirty smiles, Graeme did. He flirted with the woman sitting next to him. The only time Graeme didn't flirt was when they gave their orders to Kirsty. The woman next to Graeme tried to get Iain's attention, but he was not biting.

Kirsty came back to remove their empty plates when the woman who tried to catch Iain's attention, probably acted in desperation. When they got up to leave, she slipped a serviette in front of Iain with her phone number on it. Iain picked it up and frowned at it.

Kirsty held her breath while she waited to see what he would do. Iain looked up and caught her eyes.

Still holding her eyes, he crumbled the serviette in his hand and dropped it onto his dirty plate. Then he smiled.

And oh hell, she was *so* in trouble. That crush she thought she had on Iain? That was not a patch to what he made her feel now. She couldn't allow it. She had to remember his plan, and that was to close Joe's.

Yeah, if that would help.

That evening at Olivia's girl's night, Kirsty had to face the truth.

IAIN THOUGHT he had dealt with his newly-discovered feelings during the week. He hadn't been close. On Saturday at the Annual Veteran's Ball, he got a shock. He hadn't expected to see Kirstine there.

Aileen bumped Iain's arm, and he realised he was staring at Kirstine. Again, as he did every time she was anywhere close.

He turned towards Aileen, who was watching him with an amused grin. Iain scowled, embarrassed to be caught drooling over a woman who couldn't stand him.

Kirstine was sitting with a group of veterans, and it looked like she knew them well. She was talking and laughing at something one of them had said.

Try as he might, Iain couldn't pull his eyes away from her. She looked beautiful with her hair hanging over her shoulders. It was neither straight, nor curly, but it had a wave that made Iain itch to run his hands through it. She wore makeup tonight. Iain only then realised that she wasn't as young as she looked every day without makeup and her hair tied in a plait.

"Iain, go talk to her," Aileen whispered next to him.

Iain turned to his sister and frowned. He tried to go for the innocent look when he pretended not to know what she was talking about.

"Who are you talking about?"

"You know who I'm talking about. The woman you could hardly keep your eyes off since we've arrived," Aileen retorted, a smug smile playing around her mouth.

Iain's gaze returned to Kirstine, at the exact moment she looked up and noticed him. Her eyes widened, and after long, long moments, she looked away.

Iain heard Aileen's chuckle next to him, and he turned to look at his sister. There was no way Aileen hadn't seen that eye-lock.

"I don't know the woman, and I guess I may be the last person she would want to talk to tonight."

"You'll never know if you don't try, will you?" Aileen chuckled.

"Oh, there's your young man," Ellie said next to Kirsty.

Kirsty jumped. She hadn't realised that Ellie had taken old Major Maguire's place next to her. She had been lost in Iain's eyes for goodness how long.

She flushed and whispered, "He's not my young man."

Ellie was half deaf and the widow of one of Kirsty's grandfather's friends. What she thought was a whisper came out loud, "*Och away with you lassie.* I've seen him almost every second day at Joe's. See that look he gives you right now? He looks at you the same every time he is in Joe's. He wants to be your young man."

"You're wrong, Ellie. He's Drew Young's son, and he now owns Cairistìne Court. He wants me to move Joe's to some other place, and I refuse. He is playing some kind of weird mind game. That is the only reason he comes to Joe's. I will not budge. I'm keeping Joe's where it is," Kirsty said.

"Since when?" Major Maguire, who had returned to the table, asked.

Kirsty studied her grandfather's friends, who were all eyeing her with interest.

"The last three or four months. Iain had sent his brother and sister first and that sleazy property manager of his. Then he came himself, even after I've told him I'm not moving."

"Yet he's in Joe's a few times a week?" asked Major Maguire. "I've seen him, and like Ellie, I thought he was your suitor."

Kirsty giggled at the word suitor.

"Hardly that, Major."

"Well, even if you disagree, I still think he is interested in more than Joe's. Look, he's coming here now," Ellie whispered too loud.

Kirsty looked up. Iain was making his way towards their table. Dealing with Iain outside of Joe's was not an option.

Kirsty jumped up, making a quick excuse. She hurried to the bathroom without a backward glance. Inside, Kirsty breathed a sigh of relief. That relief was short-lived. The woman standing in front of the mirror, reapplying her lipstick, was Aileen Young. When Aileen caught Kirsty's eyes in the mirror, she smiled friendly. She turned towards Kirsty, who was still hovering in the door.

"Hiya. How are you doing?"

Kirsty moved to the washbasin and opened her purse, mumbling, "I'm good and you?"

"I'm good. It's nice to see you outside of Joe's. I love your dress," Aileen said, studying the bronze maxi dress Kirsty wore. Kirsty relaxed with Aileen's easy conversation and smiled, "Thank you. I'll tell my friend."

By the time they left the bathroom, they were talking about clothes. Kirsty gave Aileen the details of the designer who made her dress. It was an old school friend of Kirsty's and a regular at Joe's.

Kirsty hadn't expected to arrive at her table to find Iain there. He was talking to Ellie and Major Maguire.

Aileen had no other option than to introduce Aileen to her older companions.

Iain stood up. Before Kirsty knew what was going on, Major Maguire had pressured Iain to take Kirsty for the next dance. She didn't have much choice but to accept the hand Iain held out in a silent request.

She felt the heat of his hand folded around hers as they walked to the dance floor. The feeling intensified when he slid his other hand to the small of her back.

Kirsty should have known. Iain was as good a dancer as he did everything else. He didn't hold her too tight, yet his touch burned through the silky material of her dress. She had never been as aware of a man as she was with Iain. She shivered when Iain murmured her name. His burr sounded more pronounced when he did.

"Kirstine?"

Kirsty made the mistake of looking up at him. Iain's eyes were flitting over her face, his voice husky when he murmured, "You look beautiful."

Kirsty hadn't expected that. She cursed herself when she felt the flush spreading over her cheekbones. She averted her eyes, fixing them on his bowtie. She mumbled, "thank you," feeling like a moron. She hated how tongue-tied she felt in his company.

Kirsty knew she shouldn't allow it. She shouldn't let herself relax with him because she knew what he was doing. He was trying to make her soft so that she would move Joe's. That would not happen.

When the dance ended, it looked like Iain was reluctant to let her go, but Kirsty had enough. She worried that if she stayed in his arms much longer, she would succumb to his almost shy charm. When Kirsty moved away, Iain held her back, his hand firm on her arm.

"Kirstine, are you angry with me?"

Kirsty stared at him. What did he expect? He was trying to take her livelihood, her inheritance and her memories away. Yes, of course, she was angry. She reacted without thought, standing closer to him. Sarcasm dripped from every word as she growled, "Now why would I be angry with you, Mr Young? No, I'm not angry with you. I'm furious. I'm disgusted. You let your greediness ruin other people. You ride roughshod over your parents' memories by getting rid of Cairistìne Court. How can you do that? But let me tell you one thing. I'm not giving up. If you feel so little for your parents, I'll fight you till the end. I'll fight to save Joe's and I'll fight for Cairistìne Court. I owe that to your father and Joe. Have a nice life, Mr Young."

With that, Kirsty turned around and left Iain on the dance floor with a stunned expression. She didn't care if she embarrassed him.

5

Kirstine had stunned him by her accusations on Saturday night, and by Monday Iain knew he had to fix it. How he didn't know yet, but he knew it had to be something dramatic. He mulled over her words so many times he could repeat it by heart.

He realised that Joe's was more than just a business. It was the heart of a close-knit community. It was a tradition. And yes, there were many memories tied up in that place. Memories were important.

Was he selfish? He couldn't deny it. He didn't think further than getting rid of the building just to have one less thing to worry about. Aileen had mentioned that the building had carried his mother's name? Why? Why had they never heard of it or Joe's? All the questions made Iain more confused than anything else.

One thing he knew was that Dougie had been right. He had found his answer in Joe's. It might not be the answer to the original question. No, he found more than that.

Aileen knew to leave him alone. She didn't broach the subject of Kirstine on Saturday night, nor on Sunday during lunch. When Iain asked her to meet him at Joe's on Tuesday morning, Aileen had to know something was up. Iain was glad she didn't ask because he didn't know where he was going with it.

Meeting at Joe's was a bad idea. Iain struggled to concentrate on the conversation while Kirstine was in the vicinity. He only had to look at her to remember how she felt in his arms on Saturday night, and he knew he wanted more, but Kirstine didn't feel the same. It seemed like she couldn't get away from him quick enough.

He returned his gaze to his sister, who was studying him with something bordering on sympathy. Iain wasn't ready for that yet. He stood up, saying over his shoulder to Aileen, "Let's get going."

He silently followed Aileen to the entrance of Cairistìne Court with the plans in hand. He had an idea of how to win Kirstine back, but he needed to plan. All he knew he wasn't ready to give up yet. That first day he had seen Kirstine he had promised himself he would not lose the battle.

That battle he lost, but he didn't mind. Joe's would stay where it was.

This, however, was a different battle and Iain knew it had just begun. His biggest problem was how to convince Kirstine to go out with him. He didn't have a clue.

IAIN PUSHED his hands through his hair in frustration. It had been two weeks since the Veteran's Ball. He had upped his visits to Joe's, but he had made no progress with Kirstine. She was courteous enough, but not once had she smiled at him. He had tried flirting with her which felt like an alien pastime, but even that hadn't influenced her.

He couldn't even hide his interest anymore, because both his siblings had picked up on it while in the coffee shop.

He had to decide what to do with this building. He wanted to hear Aileen and Graeme's opinions before he made the final decision and asked them to meet him at Joe's. He had supposed to do it—if he could concentrate on business. With Kirstine in the vicinity, it was useless. Iain lost track of the conversation several times, and now his siblings got frustrated with him. This wouldn't do. He needed to get out of here. He got up, saying, "Let's get to work."

He turned around to pay for the coffees and bumped into someone, breathing in the scent of vanilla. Iain knew who it was, and he reached out to stop Kirstine from falling backwards. When he looked down into her wide eyes, Iain knew that this was the turning point. He needed to stop procrastinating and do something about it. Without even realising it, his hands had gentled on her shoulders. His voice sounded husky when he said, "Kirstine, I'm sorry..."

Graeme slapped Iain hard on the shoulder, roaring, "Come on, Bro'. You told us we've work to do. Oh, and you owe me. I've already settled the bill."

Iain frowned, letting his hands drop from Kirstine's shoulders. He broke eye contact and stepped around her, following his brother. Iain hadn't missed the amused look his siblings shared when he had bumped into Kirstine. It was only a matter of time before they would bring it up.

He heard Aileen's, "See you, Kirsty," and Iain frowned.

Kirsty?

How many months since he frequented Joe's and he still could not call her Kirsty? He wished he had the guts to do it. He usually had with other women, but not with her. But this was it. From now on, he would think of her as Kirsty, not Kirstine even if it is only in his mind. Maybe then he would pick up the courage to call her that.

Iain had learned many things during his visits to Joe's. He knew that Kirsty was a firm but much-adored boss. The customers loved her gentle way, and he discovered she had a soft heart. The old veterans were like family to her.

She always made sure that Ellie had something to eat. From her clothes, everyone could see that Ellie struggled financially, but she still came in most mornings when Iain was there. Each time Ellie counted the cents for a small cup of coffee. He had wondered if Ellie even had enough for that. Each time Kirsty handed over the cup and something to eat with a smile, everyone could read the gratitude in the older woman's eyes.

Ellie wasn't the only one. There had been many others over the last weeks. Take Olivia, for example, the waitress who worked on Saturdays. From what Iain could gather, she was Major Maguire's great-niece and a single mother. Olivia had a full-time job, but she worked at Joe's on Saturdays for extra cash. She got the same treatment as Ellie. Every morning she came in, got her cup of coffee and something to eat before her lift for work picked her up in front of Joe's. Since Iain heard that the tip jar was for people like Ellie and Olivia, he dropped extra cash in the jar. He made sure his siblings did the same.

Outside, Iain said to Aileen, "Take us on a tour of the building."

Aileen frowned, but at least she said nothing yet.

It didn't take them long to tour the building. It had been uncomfortable with the current tenants giving them dirty looks. They expected that. Some of them had been here for years. They didn't like that they had to move. Since Aileen had offered them the new offices, all the tenants had accepted, although some were reluctant to do it.

When they completed the tour, the three of them stood outside the building. Iain looked up at it. He asked his brother first, "What do you think?"

"Aileen was right. It's a beautiful building. It would be a shame to tear it down," Graeme murmured.

"Aileen? What do you think?" Iain asked his sister.

Aileen scowled at Iain, "I've already told you what I think. What do you want to know now, Iain?"

Iain dropped his gaze to Joe's before he turned to his brother and sister. "What do you think of us moving our offices here? Now we sold the residential portfolio, our staff pool is much smaller, and we don't need all that space. We could get more rental income for the property in Tollcross than we would get here. All three of us live on this side of Edinburgh. It would be an advantage not to struggle through traffic."

He noticed the amused glance Aileen and Graeme exchanged. He ignored it because he knew what he said appealed to them.

Graeme laughed. "Yes, Bro' and you don't have to schlep down to Leith every day to see your beautiful Kirsty."

Iain flushed, knowing that Graeme wasn't far from wrong.

Aileen first discussed business. It made Iain think Aileen had missed his attraction to Kirsty.

"I know you've done your homework and you're right. Businesswise, it would make sense. I won't miss the morning traffic into Town if we move here. I also would be happy to be working in a building that bears Mum's name."

Both brothers agreed with that sentiment. Graeme didn't hesitate and agreed to the proposed move. "I wouldn't mind being out of the city. I'm in."

Iain raised his eyebrows at Aileen, and she nodded, "I'm in."

Iain sighed relieved. "Okay, that's it then. As soon as the tenants are out, we can clean up and prepare the building for our use. I guess in about three or four months we could move. You both know what to do."

"So, big brother, when are you going to tell Kirsty that you will stop pestering about moving Joe's?" Aileen asked with her tongue in her cheek.

Iain flushed but didn't reply to that.

He already admitted that he was looking forward to his email exchange with Kirsty. As Kirsty was not talking to him other than that, he wasn't sure how to approach her. What if he told her he gave up on that idea? Would she talk to him then?

Her accusation that night at the Veteran's Ball hit hard. When did he become so cynical and hard and greedy as she accused him of being? He hated that. He had thought a lot about it. It reminded him of many of his father and grandfather's lessons over the years. The unfortunate thing was that he was still not sure what to do about it.

He sighed, "I'm not sure. She barely talks to me."

Graeme laughed. "Have you lost your touch, Bro'? I've never seen you so tongue-tied in a girl's presence. You usually have all the other women falling over your feet."

Iain glanced at Joe's again, noticing Kirsty standing at the window watching them. She probably wondered about their impromptu meeting in front of the building. He didn't look away when he answered, "Kirsty isn't like any other woman."

He didn't notice the surprise on his sibling's faces this time as his eyes were still resting on Kirsty. Yes, that was it. Kirsty wasn't like the others in his circle. She was hard-working, kind, feisty enough to stand up to him, beautiful... There were so many things he'd picked up about her, but Iain wanted to know so much more. His gut feeling told him she might be the one woman who could keep him on his toes.

KIRSTY WISHED she knew what was going on. Things had changed since that day that Iain and his siblings met in front of the building. Or she should rather say, Iain had changed. He was getting under her skin. Kirsty wasn't sure if that was a good thing.

It was as if Iain had finagled his way into Kirsty's life. He was at Joe's now every morning. He would often stop and chat with Ellie or Major Maguire. Other times he would talk to her staff, but every time he attempted to speak to Kirsty. Now it wasn't his short comment of "Surprise me," anymore. He asked about the different coffees, and Kirsty had no choice but to explain. When she described the brew she made for him that day, Iain's eyes never left her face. If she didn't know better, she could swear he was flirting with her. She shrugged it off most of the times as her imagination. This afternoon had been a prime example of that, and she couldn't ignore it. He was later than usual, only coming in after lunch. It didn't matter though. Her staff and the few regulars who recognised him greeted him like a long-lost friend. He reminded her so much of his father then as he made his way through the shop, making a joke with Major Maguire before he took his place at the counter.

Kirsty's traitorous heart beat faster when he looked straight into her eyes and smiled. Geez, he was gorgeous. She felt dizzy, and her legs weak. Was she coming down with something? How she managed to ask him what he wanted to drink was beyond her.

His eyes twinkled when he grinned, "Surprise me."

Oh, come on, she should be used to it by now, shouldn't she? Why did it have such an effect on her today?

Why? Oh hell, she knew why. She'd known it for months and tried to ignore it, hiding behind her anger because he wanted to close Joe's. Today she couldn't ignore it anymore.

Kirsty knew why she was looking forward to Iain's visits, and she had reason to worry. She had fallen so hard for him that it wasn't even funny. She hoped he didn't notice it because he might take advantage of that. She had to stay away from him. She would do it. Tomorrow.

From tomorrow.

Or maybe next week.

KIRSTY JUMPED when a voice spoke up behind her. She had just finished locking the door and had nowhere to go. There were still people milling around, but she was still worried. Her heart pounded when she turned. Her mouth dropped open when she saw who it was, "Iain? I mean, Mr Young," she stammered.

Damn, didn't she give herself a pep talk that afternoon? What was he anyway doing here?

Even in the dim light of the lamp above the door, she could see the flush creeping up his cheekbones. Iain Young here, at night, was a surprise. A blushing Iain Young was a shock.

He apologised. "I'm sorry. I didn't want to frighten you. I would like a word with you, please?"

No, no, no, no. She wasn't ready for this. She didn't have the energy for this. Not tonight. Especially not tonight. She was feeling way too vulnerable for it.

She lifted her chin, muttering, "I told you to talk to my lawyer."

He shook his head. "No, it's not about... Please, I would like to talk to you outside of Joe's. It's awkward, but... Please, have something to drink with me?" he pleaded.

Kirsty frowned. What was this?

Should she go with him? No, she should rephrase it. Could she go with him, without making a fool of herself? She already felt like a schoolgirl with her first crush whenever he was near, but when she looked into his pleading eyes, Kirsty found herself nodding her agreement. It seemed that she had no willpower around him.

She shivered when he took her arm to lead her across the street. They went to the same bar down the road where she had seen him only a few weeks ago.

It was the time between the after-work crowd leaving, and before the evening punters arrived. They had no trouble finding a place in a quiet corner. The waitress who came to take their order ignored Kirsty, and her eyes fixed on Iain. He might be so used to women fawning over him he didn't notice it. He ignored the waitress' flirty looks and asked Kirsty, "What would you like to drink?"

"A glass of red wine, please."

He nodded and studied the menu. "Chianti fine with you or do you prefer something else?" he asked Kirsty.

Kirsty had been studying him, admiring the sharp lines of his face. When he asked her all of a sudden, turning those intense blue eyes to her, she hit a blank. At least she heard his suggestions and mumbled, "Chianti is fine, thank you."

He put the menus to the side and said to the waitress, "Two glasses of Chianti, please."

He surprised her. Most of the guys she dated before wouldn't touch wine. Too girly for them she suspected. Iain had no such qualms. Some, like her asshole ex, insisted on the most expensive whisky to impress his friends.

What further surprised her was that Iain still ignored the waitresses' flirtatious glances. He was friendly but not overly so. He was also not condescending, which was a point in his favour. Not that he needed any more.

As soon as the woman brought their order, Iain thanked her and turned to Kirsty. When their eyes met, a blush spread over her cheeks. At least the soft light in the pub camouflaged most of it.

Iain's eyes looked softer tonight than it had that first time Kirsty had seen him. His hair was still messy and the blue eyes as penetrating, but tonight there was an added ingredient. There was a twinkle in his eyes and a sexy curl around his lips.

Iain held his glass towards her and Kirsty raised hers. His smile broadened when he clinked his glass against hers.

Iain lifted the glass to his nose, smelled the aroma and took a tentative sip as he had that first day with the latte. When he swallowed, his eyes met hers again.

Kirsty took a big gulp of her wine, nothing as refined as when he did it. Geez, you would've thought she didn't know how to drink wine. And she did. Olivia had, since she returned to Edinburgh, taught Kirsty and Morag enough about wine tasting. Not that it helped tonight.

Iain might not have noticed. He had a completely different expression on his face when he looked at her. She felt more heat spreading through her.

To break the sudden tension, she asked, "You wanted to talk to me?"

Iain took another sip of his wine, but Kirsty could have sworn he was blushing. He nodded. "Yes, as I said, this is a discussion for outside Joe's."

Kirsty frowned, and Iain explained, "I've heard a rumour about your tip jars."

"What rumour?" Kirsty frowned.

"That you use the tip money to give coffee and something to eat to people who couldn't afford it. Is that true?"

"Yes, that's true. My grandfather had started it when he opened Joe's."

Iain frowned. "And if there isn't enough money in the tip jars? What do you do?"

Kirsty took a sip of her wine before she answered. "Depending on who it is, I carry it myself, but I can't do it for every person who needs it."

Iain nodded. "Ellie is one you help?"

Kirstine frowned. "Yes, but how did you know?"

Iain smiled.

"I've spent enough time in Joe's to notice these things."

"So why are you so interested in this?" Kirsty asked.

Iain flushed, but then he met her eyes. "Because I would like to contribute so you could help more people. I know it's something small, but sometimes the small things mean more than big gestures. Also, I feel as if it was something my father would have done."

Kirsty admitted, "He did."

Iain took a deep breath and nodded. "Then you'll allow me to continue something my father did?"

When Kirsty nodded, Iain smiled. "How did he do it? I mean, I could leave cash in the jar, but it might be too obvious and even be a risk."

"Every week Drew would leave an envelope with cash in it. Sometimes it was a hundred pounds, and sometimes it was fifty. It was more than enough to help Ellie and the others to have at least one meal a day."

"Then that's what I'll do," Iain decided. He still urged Kirsty, "Will you tell me if you need more?"

"If you want to," Kirsty agreed.

While they were drinking their wine, Iain asked more questions about Joe's. To Kirsty's surprise, she relaxed, but she still worried that she would relax too much and would enjoy Iain's company. For that reason, she declined a second glass of wine or his offer to take her home.

The following morning Iain was back at Joe's. He slipped an envelope across the counter to Kirsty when she brought his order. Kirsty nodded and went to put it in the safe. She would count it later.

The following week, Iain surprised her again when he waited for her outside Joe's. His excuse? He wanted to talk to her.

Kirsty watched him with scepticism written over her face. Like the last time, they walked the short distance to the pub in silence. After the waitress had served their drinks, Kirsty asked, "So what do you want to talk about tonight?"

6

Iain grimaced. "Again, it is an awkward situation."

Kirsty frowned, "What is?"

"Olivia," he admitted.

"What about Olivia?" Kirsty frowned.

"Major Maguire told me that Olivia is a single mum. I know she had a full-time job but also worked for you on Saturdays. This week she had been in Joe's most afternoons. What's up? Did she lose her job?"

Kirsty shook her head, "No, but the company she and Morag's fiancée are working for struggle. They've already let some staff go. Olivia and Peter still have their jobs, but the company reduced their hours which mean less pay. Peter is fine. He works part-time at a call centre, but Livvie can't do that. She can only work when she can get a babysitter. Some older ladies like Ellie help her out, but sometimes Mattias, her son, gets sick and she has to take care of him. Not all employers understand it."

"What does she do?" Iain asked.

"She's an interior designer. She designs the interior of restaurants and pubs, but she'd done other odd jobs too, like working as a barista or a sommelier all over the world.

"There are few jobs available for people with those skills in Edinburgh," Iain surmised.

Kirsty nodded, "Yes, that's the truth."

Iain rubbed his cheek. It looked like he was thinking hard, but then he decided. He leaned forward to Kirsty, "I may give her a job. My assistant needs an assistant. It's not much, but it will help to pay the bills. I guess, as a designer she knows graphics programmes. There are a few things we're working on where her skills may come in handy. I'll even provide her with a laptop if she doesn't have one, so she can work at home when her child is sick."

He pulled out his wallet and took out a business card, "Let her contact me.

Kirsty took the card, playing with it when she frowned at Iain, "Why didn't you give it to her yourself? You could have spoken to her this afternoon?"

Iain lifted his hand and wiped over his mouth. He looked nervous—and embarrassed. His next words shocked Kirsty because that was the last thing she had expected.

"Would you believe that it was an excuse to see you?"

Kirsty flushed. "Why do you want to do that?"

Iain chuckled, "When last have you looked in the mirror? You are a beautiful woman, Kirsty. I took months to work up the courage to ask you. I figured that after our first couple of meetings, I am the last guy you would want to date. After what you said at the Veteran's Ball..."

Kirsty flushed, "I'm sorry. I was rude."

Iain shook his head. "It was time I heard a few home truths. I promise... Wait, I said I would not talk business. I had hoped... I would like you to get to know me so you can see I'm not such a bad person. I would like to get to know you, Kirsty."

Kirsty frowned confused, "I don't understand. Many other women are throwing themselves at you. Look at that wait-ress. She can't keep her eyes off you, inspecting you as if you're a lump of meat. I've seen the other women in Joe's. I've seen your photo in the gossip columns. They're beauti-ful, smart, and everything a guy like you needs. I'm a barista. I'm nothing special."

"Never say that again, Kirsty," Iain scowled. You are special. You are beautiful. You are smart and kind d hard-working and loyal. I don't know about the funny yet, but I hope to find out soon," he added.

Iain's hand slipped over Kirsty's. He moved closer to her, his voice urgent, "Don't believe everything you read in the papers, Kirsty. I'm not that person they make me out to be. And no, I don't want those women. Trust me, I've tried, but that lifestyle isn't for me. Yes, I may have money, but I like simple stuff. I don't want someone who likes to go out club-bing every night and get noticed. I want someone who understands that I have a business to run and work long hours. Someone I can talk to over a glass of wine as we had tonight and last week. I want someone who won't mind going for a walk on the beach, even if the wind is blowing. I want someone with whom I can watch old movies or just talk to in front of the fire or with whom I can discover new places. I want someone with whom I can be myself and not pretend that I'm in control when I'm not. Call me crazy, but I have a feeling that you are the woman with whom I can do these things. Please give me a chance, Kirsty. I want to get to know you better."

Kirsty tried to take in everything he said. When he spoke, it was as if she was with him, from the walk on the beach and everything else. She wanted it too, and she wanted to do it with Iain.

She studied Iain's face the same way he was examining her while he waited for her answer.

Kirsty had already accepted at the funeral, and again earlier that afternoon that she'd fallen for Iain. She hadn't dreamed that he felt this attraction too. It scared her, but before her fears could prevent her from agreeing, she nodded, "Okay."

Iain grinned, a beautiful smile pulling at the corners of his mouth and eyes. For the first time, Kirsty returned Iain's smile.

He surprised her when he lifted her hand to his mouth and brushed his lips against her knuckles. Kirsty shivered when she felt the heat of his hand and mouth against her skin. Iain might have had the same reaction as he tightened his grip around hers and his eyes darkened.

This sudden and intense awareness was overwhelming. Kirsty hoped it would be worth the heartache. She knew that would follow when, whatever this was between them, had run its course.

The rest of the evening went by in a blur. They talked a lot while they had dinner and finished a bottle of wine. Kirsty hadn't realised that they had so many interests in common.

Throughout the evening, Iain's hand touched her often. It made her more aware of him than she had been of any other man before him. He was an attentive date, giving her all his attention.

Later that evening, Iain took her home. He even held her hand when he walked her to her door, his driver waiting at the curb. Iain waited for her to open the door, then he bent, brushed his lips over her cheek so softly she thought she had imagined it. The next moment he uttered a quick good-night and hurried away as if he couldn't get away from her fast enough.

Watching him go, Kirsty felt disappointed. She wanted him to kiss her. For goodness sake, she had been fantasising about it for months now. Tonight she thought it would happen at last.

That night while she got ready for bed, Kirsty thought about the evening and her feelings for Iain. After tonight she had to accept that what she felt that day next to Drew's grave, had morphed from a crush to love.

KIRSTY HADN'T EXPECTED to see Iain again so soon. He surprised her when he walked into Joe's the next morning. This time she didn't miss the open admiration in his eyes and the flirty way he spoke to her.

It disappointed her when he glanced at his watch and grimaced. He got up to settle his bill before he came back to

Kirsty and asked, "Is there a place we could talk in private?"

Kirsty was aware of the curious glances of her staff when she led him to her office. As soon as they entered, Iain closed the door behind him. Before Kirsty knew what was to come, he pressed her against the door, and his mouth captured hers.

The kiss was everything Kirsty had dreamed about last night. It changed from sweet and soft to hot and all-consuming back to gentle and tender again. Without even knowing it, Kirsty's hands had crept around his neck, burying her fingers in the short hair just above his collar.

When they pulled apart, they were both breathing hard. Iain let his head drop to Kirsty's shoulder, and he managed through ragged breaths, "I wanted to kiss you last night. I should have done it. I tortured myself the whole night, dreaming about kissing you like this."

Kirsty chuckled, "You were not the only one."

Iain lifted his head, returning her smile, "That's good to know."

He brushed his mouth lightly against hers and stepped back. "I would like to stay here, but I have a meeting. May I see you tonight?"

Kirsty nodded and stepped away from the door. She laughed when he opened the door and blew her a kiss before he disappeared around the corner. A minute later he was back, his look sheepish when he admitted, "I forgot to ask for your number," while he pulled out his phone.

Kirsty watched while he punched in the numbers, still a bit stunned about that kiss.

Iain looked up at her and grinned when he put his phone away, but the next moment his smile disappeared. With a groan, he cupped her cheek with his hand, swooping his head down to claim her mouth in yet another devastating kiss.

Footsteps in the hallway caused them to break apart. Kirsty's legs felt as if they couldn't hold her. She leaned against her desk while Iain disappeared for the second time around the corner. She picked up her phone, pretending to study it when Morag appeared in the doorway. Kirsty didn't look up when Morag asked, "Sorry, when do you expect the new order?"

Kirsty answered, "This morning." She only then lifted her head to add, "Could you keep an eye out for it, please? I'll be here for a while doing the books."

She didn't miss Morag's knowing smile but ignored it when her phone beeped with a new message. It was from Iain. Kirsty could feel the butterflies in her tummy when she read, "*Hey beautiful. Can't wait to see you tonight. Seven, your apartment?*"

Kirsty echoed his feelings but only answered with one word.

"*Yes.*"

She didn't know where this was going with Iain, but she would enjoy the ride.

WHAT STARTED as two dates the first week became three the following week. In the weeks since then, they had seen each other almost every day. Sometimes Iain had to travel for business or attend a business function. It scared Kirsty how much she missed him then.

Some nights they would stay in at Kirsty's apartment. They might order something in while they watched television or a movie. Other times they would try out a new recipe together. Some of them were masterpieces, but others were total disasters. It didn't matter though. It was fun.

Once a week Iain took Kirsty out on a proper dinner date, as he called it. Some Saturdays they might go for those walks on the beach or in a park as Iain had mentioned. One or two evenings they would take in a show or a movie, whatever they were in the mood for. It didn't matter to Iain. He guarded his time with Kirsty almost with jealousy.

It was refreshing to find a woman comfortable in her skin, who enjoyed eating as much as he did and loved trying new dishes. For the first time in his life, Iain loved spending so much time with a woman, doing ordinary, mundane things.

Kirsty had even helped Iain to purchase a good coffee machine and taught him to make his own brew. His siblings thought it hilarious when they went to visit him for the visit time after he had the machine, and he had shown off his new skills. They had known of Iain's former aversion to coffee.

His moment of truth had come a month after they had started dating. Kirsty hadn't been working that Saturday, and they took a day trip away from the city, down the coastal road to the East Neuk of Fife. They stopped at all the small villages along the way to explore. The weather played along that day.

Iain had allowed himself one luxury since they sold the portion of Young's. He bought himself a sky-blue BMW roadster, and for the first time since he received it the previous month, Iain could enjoy the car. When they put the roof down, Kirsty hadn't even complained that her hair was getting messy. She tied it in a loose plait and laughed when the wind kept on pulling strings out.

They bought fish and chips in Anstruther and ate them on a bench overlooking the Harbour Beach. When they finished eating, Kirsty licked the greasiness from her fingers with a laugh. That was the defining moment for Iain.

He loved her.

The truth came quietly, filling his heart and his head. It didn't even surprise Iain. He probably had known all along.

He kissed her, ignoring the greasiness that clung to their hands and mouths, probably surprising Kirsty with the intensity of his kiss. It was as if he wanted to convey his feelings to her. He hoped it wasn't his imagination, but Kirsty's kisses made Iain feel as if she returned his feelings.

Iain had been right when he first convinced Kirsty to go out with him. She was entirely different from all the women he had ever dated. None of them would have enjoyed eating greasy fish and chips with their hands. They would have wanted to eat in the most expensive hotels or places where people would have noticed them. They wouldn't walk barefoot on the beach with him. They would have hated to get their hair messed up when he put the roof down to enjoy the full rays of the sun.

That night, driving home, Iain planned. He wanted a future with Kirsty. She was the woman he would like to wake up with every day until the day he would no longer lift his head.

KIRSTY AND IAIN, like most locals, waited for August to begin —and end. The city was far busier during this month, and it had nothing to do with the weather. The temperatures were the warmest than they were the whole year. They had several days of sunshine, but that wasn't it.

Edinburgh in August was like nowhere else in the world. Thousands of artists and performers for the annual festival arrived in the city then. The Royal Mile was buzzing with street performers and festivalgoers.

The city came alive, and it was often one of the busiest months for Kirsty—even though she was out of the way in Leith.

Iain was one local who complained about the busier, heaving streets. It made the day-to-day running of his business more difficult. If he couldn't walk to a meeting, he didn't have one. It was as simple as that.

Iain had heeded his siblings and his PA's advice and hadn't tried to negotiate the streets late afternoon. He went into the office earlier, left before lunch, and sometimes even worked from home—or in Joe's.

He scheduled most of his meetings out of the City. When it became too much, he left to visit the offices in other parts of Scotland.

Kirsty hadn't escaped the influx of visitors but she, unlike Iain, wasn't complaining. She didn't have to negotiate the traffic as she walked to Joe's.

Most festivalgoers stayed in the city. In recent years, some had ventured to the fringe venues in Leith. Leith Walk was busier than usual, but for Kirsty, it was an exciting and busy time. She had to hire a few students to serve and assist the chef. That would allow the barista and chef to concentrate on the more essential tasks.

Some of Joe's regular customers complained that it was impossible to go out in the City. They said they struggled to get a table for lunch, and when they did, the restaurant had inflated the prices. Kirsty didn't make the mistake of increasing her prices for the festival. Most of her clientele were locals, and they were the ones who would support Joe's when the festival was over. She didn't want to alienate them.

Even though Joe's benefited, Kirsty could understand why the locals got fed up. Those working anywhere between Princess Street and the Royal Mile complained the most. One of her regular Saturday customers said 'the novelty of seeing the shows soon wears off'. He grumbled that if one comedienne pressed another flier in his hand, he would not be responsible for his actions. He met that comedienne on his way down to Waverley station every day.

OVER THE WEEKS he and Kirsty had seen each other, they had several long talks. Before they dated, he'd hoped to learn more about Kirsty and her life, and he did. He listened and stored that information because one day, he might need it. It now came in handy.

Since he realised that he loved Kirsty, Iain had to stop himself several times when he wanted to blurt out his feelings. It scared him. It was too soon even though he knew he couldn't compare what was between him and Kirsty to any of his previous relationships. This was so much more.

Somewhere in the back of his mind, he still had a niggling fear he was rushing things as he did before. He didn't want to mess this up with Kirsty. This was too important. Iain knew that Kirsty was his forever love. What if Kirsty didn't believe him if he told her now he loved her? It was stupid, but Iain couldn't help it. That fear was preventing him from saying how he felt.

Iain thought if he couldn't say the words yet, he could convey his feelings with actions. Even though he grumbled about the inconvenience the festival caused him, he knew Kirsty loved it. He would do anything for her and called in a few favours.

Iain cut down on his workload for the last week of the festival. Feeling more relaxed, he took Kirsty to some venues in Leith to listen to music. On one of those evenings, they drifted back to the pub where he had first asked her to go out with him. When they each had a glass of wine in hand, Iain cleared his throat, "I have a surprise for you."

Kirsty smiled, "You know I love surprises."

Iain brushed his mouth over hers and grinned, "I know you do. I need to warn you, though. This may make you sad, so if you don't want to accept it, I will understand."

Kirsty's smile disappeared, "What do you mean?"

Iain breathed in and exhaled before he said, "I know how close you were with your grandfather. You've told me so much about him, and I wish I had known him too."

Kirsty nodded, still waiting for Iain's surprise. "You've told me you and Joe went to the Tattoo every year."

Kirsty nodded, "We did. I've tried to ignore all the hype in the last few weeks. It makes me sad that he won't be here this year. It is the first year…"

"I know," Iain admitted. "That is why I… I got tickets for the Tattoo. Not only for the two of us but if you'd like, we could invite Ellie and Major Maguire too. That is if you want to go. If you don't, I'll understand."

When Kirsty's eyes filled with tears, Iain felt terrible. He put his arm around her shoulders and pulled her against his chest. His hand rubbed over her hair and back while he mumbled, "I'm so sorry. I didn't want to make you cry."

Kirsty lifted her head. With tears still running down her cheeks, she smiled, "No, Iain. Don't apologise."

She put his hand on his cheek and said, "Yes, I'm sad that my grandfather won't be here to see it, but I'm happy too. Thank you for thinking about it. Thank you for getting the tickets and inviting Major Maguire and Ellie too. I'm crying because you are so thoughtful."

"Are you sure?" Iain pressed.

She nodded, "I'm sure, Iain. Thank you."

To Iain's surprise, Kirsty pulled his head down and kissed him. He could taste the salt of her tears, mingled with the wine on her lips. At that moment, Iain knew he would do anything for her. If he had to choose between his wealth and Kirsty, he would pick her. Every time.

That was when Iain also knew what he had to do with Joe's. He'd mulled over it for the last few weeks. He was looking for a big gesture to prove to Kirsty how much she meant to him.

He had just found his answer.

Now was not the moment to discuss it, though. Iain lifted his mouth from hers and stared into her eyes, willing her to see how much he cared.

Kirsty smiled, and Iain smiled back relieved. When he talked again, he sat back with his arm still around her shoulders and said, "Okay, that's settled then. We'll tell them tomorrow?"

When Kirsty nodded, Iain asked, "Do you think they will be up for an early dinner before the Tattoo? It doesn't have to be anything fancy. You know what kind of place they would like."

Kirsty glanced around her and said, "I know they like it here. Would you mind coming here for dinner?"

Iain shook his head, "No, I don't. Since this is where you agreed to go out with me, it has become my favourite place."

He laughed when Kirsty blushed but changed the subject, "I have another surprise for you."

Kirsty turned her head sideways and smiled, "You're full of surprises tonight, aren't you?"

Iain chuckled, "I am, and I'll have a few more for you before the year is out."

"Oh, yes?" she smiled.

Iain brushed his mouth over hers in a brief kiss. When he pulled back, he nodded, "Oh, yes. But let's talk about this one first. Would you like to go on a picnic on Monday in Princess Street Gardens? As you know, it is the last evening of the festival, with a concert and fireworks display."

Kirsty's eyes widened, "You still got tickets?"

Iain nodded, "Well, Moira did. I don't know how she did it, but she got us tickets. She even got Priority Entry tickets that allow us entry to the Garden before the gates open. We'll be able to find a nice spot before the other hundreds of people arrive."

"That would be great. If you haven't planned the food yet, I can pack a basket for us."

Iain flushed, "I hoped you would offer. And I hope it will include some of your chicken mayonnaise sandwiches and chocolate brownies."

Kirsty laughed, "I should have known. You only date me for my food."

Iain teased, "Not only your food, Love. For your coffee too."

Kirsty slapped his arm, and Iain laughed. He leaned closer again and said against her lips, "And the way you make me laugh."

He brushed his mouth again over hers, "And the way you make me feel."

Another brief kiss followed before he said, "And the way you kiss."

This time he prolonged the kiss. If he hadn't, he would have said so much more.

7

K irsty looked up when she heard the rap on the door. She smiled when she saw it was Iain. As usual, when she saw him, her heart beat faster. She hurried to the door and unlocked it.

She hadn't expected Iain tonight. He was meeting two of his school friends, and she wondered if he cancelled it.

Iain rushed in, bringing with him a gust of wind and cold air. Kirsty closed the door in a hurry, not wanting to make Joe's more frozen than it already was. Iain leaned back and locked the door. The way he looked at her, a broad smile plastered on his face, made her legs weak. He was such a gorgeous man, and when he smiled? Ooh, those are the times she wanted to grab him. She loved when he was like this. There was no sign of the serious businessman she'd seen for the first time here in Joe's. No, now there was mischief in his eyes, and he smiled more often.

Kirsty had been so caught up in his eyes and smile. She hadn't noticed that he had kept his one hand behind his back until he brought it out. In his hand he clutched a bunch of pink and white lisianthus, the petals glistening with raindrops.

Kirsty took it, burying her face in the flowers, breathing in the delicate fragrance. Iain had learned his lesson when he sent her flowers the first time. The sweet smell of the lilies he'd chosen had her sneezing the whole evening, much to his chagrin. Kirsty looked up and smiled, "What did I do to deserve this?"

Iain smiled, "For being you."

He fingered one of the pink petals and said, "They reminded me of you. Graceful. Feminine. Elegant."

Kirsty flushed with pleasure, "Thank you. For the flowers and the compliment." She looked down at the flowers in her hand. Iain was right. They looked feminine, and she had to admit: she liked the thought that Iain saw her like that.

When Iain stepped closer, Kirsty looked up at him. Their eyes held, and then Iain lifted his hand to stroke one finger over her cheek. He took another step while still keeping her eyes. Kirsty held her breath, feeling the anticipation building.

Iain took the flowers back from Kirsty and put it on the counter behind her. His hand on her cheek slid behind her neck, the other on her hip, and then he lowered his head. It felt as if it happened in slow motion, but then his lips touched hers, brushing over hers. Kirsty thought she imagined the kiss as it had been so brief.

Iain's eyes still held hers when he did it again, brushing his lips against hers—once, twice and then a third time. Each time, he lingered longer on her lips, and the time between them became shorter. One last time she could feel his breath fanning across her face before he claimed her mouth. This time, the kiss was so much more.

Kirsty sighed, opening her mouth beneath his. The kiss changed in an instant to mirror their first kiss in her office. She slid her hands in Iain's hair, giving herself over to his probing lips and tongue.

A loud rap on the door had them pull apart. Iain groaned between shuddering breaths.

"Geez, that's bad timing."

He glanced at the door with regret and said to Kirsty, "That must be my friends, Rab and Duncan. I know we didn't have plans for tonight, but I would like to introduce you to them. Please come with us to the pub?"

Kirsty knew his friends wouldn't have been able to see into Joe's, but she still blushed. "Are you sure?" she asked.

"I'm sure. I would have introduced you before, but they were both away."

"Okay then, let me put this in water and then I'll lock up," Kirsty agreed, picking up the flowers.

"Okay, I'll tell them to meet us there," Iain said over his shoulder while he went to unlock the door.

Kirsty rushed to her office to pick up the vase and get her bag. She switched off the lights in the office and took the vase and flowers to the kitchen. She arranged them in the vase and filled it with water. She joined Iain a few minutes later. He already had her coat in his hands.

By the time they arrived at the pub, Kirsty's cheeks felt flushed from the cold wind that whipped around the corners. She was glad she had kept her hair in the plait as she would have been a real mess. That wasn't how she wanted to meet Iain's friends for the first time.

She tried to hide her sudden bout of nerves from Iain. Kirsty must admit that she had wondered why she never met his friends. When Iain spoke, she looked at him in surprise. He looked nervous too. Somehow that thought reassured her, even though it might sound ridiculous. He had nothing to worry about.

"You may have noticed by now I'm not as easy going as my siblings. They are the heart and soul of a party. Not me. I have a few close friends I feel comfortable socialising with like Rab and Duncan. They were my best friends since we met at Prep. I hope you like them."

"Why wouldn't I?" Kirsty asked.

He shrugged, "I don't know."

They couldn't continue their discussion as they reached the pub.

Kirsty soon learned that those nerves were unnecessary. Iain's friends were as easy to get along with as he was. They were so down to earth that it surprised Kirsty when she learned what they did. Rab was a medical doctor with Doctors without Borders, and Duncan recently became an associate professor in International Relations at Edinburgh University. As Duncan pointed out, they were the three biggest geeks at school. Kirsty shook her head, "I don't believe that for one minute."

All three laughed, "Well, that's true. Our school had a Geek Club. Rab was our President," Iain admitted.

"So what did you do?"

"Well, we played computer games and had movie nights or quiz nights. Nothing exciting, but it had been fun," Rab said. "It was more of an excuse to socialise."

"Hm, and Rab and Duncan still hadn't grown out of their quiz nights. They go to every pub quiz in Edinburgh when they get a chance. I'm warning you, they are always hunting for team members," Iain said to Kirsty.

For the next hour, the three friends teased each other, while they regaled Kirsty with stories of their childhood. Kirsty had to admit that she had a far more enjoyable evening than she expected.

After her second glass of wine, Kirsty leaned into Iain and whispered, "I will leave now."

He looked disappointed, "Do you have to?"

Kirsty nodded. "Yes, catch up. You haven't seen each other for a while."

Rab and Duncan had both been away over the summer. Rab had been working in Asia with Doctors without Borders and Duncan went to visit a cousin in Australia.

Iain glanced at his two friends before he turned to Kirsty, "Okay, but then I'd like to see you tomorrow night."

"Yeah, that's fine."

She stood up, smiling to Rab and Duncan, "It was great meeting you."

They both stood up, and to her surprise, they both hugged her as if they were old friends. Iain put his hand on her back and said to his friends over his shoulder, "You can order in the meantime. I'll be back soon."

The cold wind hit her in the face as Kirsty came outside. She now wished she had waited inside for her cab. Or maybe not.

Iain pulled her close, and without preamble, he lowered his head and kissed her. It was only the beep of the cabbie's horn that tore them apart.

In a daze, Kirsty got in the cab while Iain held the door open for her. He leaned in, brushed his mouth over hers and whispered, "See you tomorrow, Beautiful."

Kirsty ignored the cabbie's knowing grin.

Iain didn't miss his friends' amused smiles when he returned to the table. They both studied him for so long that Iain shifted in his seat.

"I don't know if the pink suit you," Rab teased. "I would have thought red is more your colour."

Iain flushed. They knew what he and Kirsty did when he was outside. He took his handkerchief out of his pocket and wiped his mouth.

"So?" Duncan asked, "This is now the Kirsty you couldn't stop talking about all summer."

Iain nodded.

"I'm curious," Rab probed. "What have you bought for her?"

Iain snorted, "I'm trying, guys. It is difficult but would you believe me that the most money I've spent on her so far was tickets to the Tattoo?"

They both gaped at him, "No jewellery or expensive holidays or a car or something?"

Iain shook his head.

"Nothing? Are you serious?" Rab asked.

"Then you must have told her how you feel. I bet you did," Rab insisted.

Iain again shook his head, "Nothing. There were so many times I've almost told her I loved her, but then I think, no, it is too soon. And the weirdest thing is with Kirsty it doesn't feel too soon, but I can't risk it. Not with her. I need to make sure because I don't want to hurt her. She's..."

Iain swallowed, "I'm ninety-nine-point-nine-nine percent sure she is the one. It is only that tiny bit of doubt that stops me from saying so. What if I make a mistake again? What if I'm too hasty? Geez, guys, you know me. You know how easily I've fallen in love before only to realise that it was not the real thing. It's all a mess then and I... I can't risk it with Kirsty. This is too important."

Duncan leaned back in his chair and said, "You know what I think?"

Iain snorted, "No, but you will tell me anyway."

Duncan's mouth curled up in a smile, "True. Iain, yes, we know you. We know how fast you fall for a woman. We know that when you fall, you will do anything to impress a woman. That had always been your downfall. But I can tell you the little I've seen of Kirsty tonight, is that she differs greatly from the girls you've dated before. I don't think your money or your wealth impress her at all. She looks like the woman who would value your love and attention far more than any flashy presents."

Iain nodded. "That's true. That is why I know she's *The One*. She is so different from all the other women in the past. With her... I don't have to show off. I don't have to be a big hot-shot lawyer or businessman. Geez, guys. You know me better than anyone, even my siblings. You know that if I had the opportunity, I would rather sit in front of the fire and read a book than socialise. Being wealthy is nice. It's nice to have a beautiful house and a car and to do whatever I want. But that is not what defines me. With Kirsty, I can be me, and that feels great."

Rab snorted, "We've noticed. It's great to see you acting so natural with a woman. You could be a pain in the arse before when you dated a new woman."

Iain flushed. He knew Rab was right. He looked up when Rab asked, "What makes Kirsty so different? Why do you feel you can be yourself with her?"

Iain had thought about it for a while now, but he still didn't know the answer. He shook his head, "I'm not sure. It might be because I didn't jump in immediately. Hell, I took months before I asked her out. In that time I saw the person she was. And I liked what I saw. I mean not only her looks. She's everything I admire in a woman. She's beautiful, feisty, hardworking, empathetic, intelligent... I can go on and on. I can talk to her for hours and hours without noticing the time pass by. I can do things with her I haven't done with any other woman before."

Iain looked up at his friends and said, "We all grew up wealthy. We all had privileged lifestyles. We're used to travelling overseas and living in five-star hotels or resorts. We're used to eating in Michelin-starred restaurants. These months with Kirsty showed me how much fun it could be to do normal stuff like any other couple in the country. It's nice to go for a walk on the beach or have a picnic in the park. It's nice to have fish and chips out of newspaper wrappings, licking your fingers afterwards. The nicest meals I ate the last few months were not at the fancy restaurants. It's driving out of the city and finding a small country pub or a little-known Italian restaurant on a side street. It's those meals Kirsty and I cooked in her kitchen and the sandwiches she makes for a picnic. It made me realise that we've lived in such a bubble we missed out on small, real things in life."

Rab nodded, "I know what you mean. My time with Doctors without Borders had shown me a different side of life. I appreciate what we have so much more when I come back. And I agree, it's not the luxuries I crave when I am away. I'm just happy to have a mattress or a hot shower or meal. I would like to think it made me a better person but not better than other people. It made me see things and people differently. As you said, we lived in a bubble. We only associated with people with the same background than we had or went to school with or to university. It's nice, you know?"

Iain nodded, "Yes, it is."

Both Iain and Rab looked at Duncan, who was listening to them, but he had a faraway look in his eyes. Rab nudged him, "It seems both Iain and I had a few enlightening experiences this summer. What about you?"

Duncan flushed. He shrugged, "I might have, and no, I'm not spilling my guts. Not yet, anyway. I'll tell you when I figured things out."

Neither Rab nor Iain argued as they knew Duncan. That was who he was. Duncan anyway didn't give Iain a chance to say anything. He asked, "It all sounds nice. You know, how you are with Kirsty and the things you do. You look comfortable with each other, but please tell me there is more between you than that."

Iain could feel the flush creeping up his face. He drew his lower lip between his teeth while he wondered if he should confess. At last, he said, "You may not believe me, but... Even though the chemistry is off the charts, we haven't taken it any further. For the same reasons I haven't told her how I felt, I'm scared of messing it up. Hell, I've been a saint these last few months. I can't tell you through how many long runs and cold showers I suffered. But, to tell you the truth, I don't know how much longer I can wait."

Rab and Duncan looked at each other and then Rab laughed, "Now we don't have to wonder any more. We know Kirsty got you tamed. All I want to know is, what are you going to do about it?"

Iain grimaced, "I don't want to wait much longer. That is why I wanted you to meet her tonight. I wanted to find out if... I guess if you see what I see with Kirsty. That she's different. It still worried me that I'm making the same stupid mistakes as in the past. If you see what I see, I can move forward."

Duncan nodded, "I don't think you're making a mistake, Iain."

Rab nodded, "Me neither. I'd say go for it."

Iain exhaled, "Thanks, guys."

He laughed, "Not that I needed your approval, but it's good to know that you agree with me."

"So, what are you going to do?" Duncan insisted.

Iain frowned, "I don't know yet. I'm still not going to rush into anything. I thought I'll introduce her to my lifestyle, and I want her to get to know you and my siblings. And then I may need a big gesture to prove to her how much I love her. I know... You don't have to tell me she may not need it, but you don't know the whole story."

He glanced at Rab, "Remember that night we were here in the pub before you left for your latest stint in Asia? We were talking about Joe's and that Joe's may have to close?"

Rab nodded, "Yes, wasn't it something about the owner of the building wanting Kirsty to move?"

Iain grimaced, "Yes, and I own the building. It was me..."

Rab's mouth fell open, "Are you serious? Why? I mean, why do you want to close the building?"

Iain sighed and told them what happened before, and the big reveal he was still hiding from Kirsty.

Duncan shook his head when Iain finished speaking. "I hope you keeping it a secret will not backfire, Iain."

Iain sure as hell hoped so too.

8

While driving to Joe's late on Saturday afternoon, Iain wondered what had happened. It felt as if summer had disappeared overnight. It was autumn already. The trees lining the capital's streets had turned a beautiful golden brown, adding a splash of colour to the otherwise grey city. But then, he didn't have to think too hard about what had happened to July and August or even the early days of September. He chuckled when he remembered his grandfather's expression, 'time flies when you're having a good time.'

His grandfather wasn't wrong. For the first time in years, Iain had enjoyed the long summer days, but he knew it all had to do with Kirsty. Doing things with her had been fun and relaxing. It had been so different from his previous relationships. With Kirsty, Iain did something instead of standing on the outside looking in.

Leaving his car, he felt the bite in the air already. Soon winter would hit them in full force.

The light in Joe's was still on, but the 'Closed' sign was on the door. Kirsty wanted to finish her admin after she closed, and Iain, although reluctant, had given her the time. He hoped she had finished by now. He hadn't seen her for two days as he had been in Aberdeen.

Iain rapped on the door, and a few seconds later, Kirsty unlocked it. Iain barely gave her a chance to open it before he pulled her into his arms. Their kiss was hungry, and it took Iain a while before he pulled away to say hello.

Breathing deep, Kirsty pulled him inside and locked the door behind him.

"I'm almost done. Do you want a coffee while I finish up?"

Iain nodded. "Yes, sure. I can pour myself a cup by now. Do what you need to do. Do you also want one?"

Kirsty shook her head.

"No, I poured a cup before you came. I need to lock up the back, and when you poured your coffee, I'll clean up the machine."

Kirsty took a sip of her coffee and disappeared into her office. Iain listened to her movements while he poured the coffee while he took his usual space at the counter. He hadn't finished his coffee before Kirsty came back and switched off the machine. She made quick work of cleaning up. When she finished, she sat down next to Iain with her mug cradled between her hands.

Iain smiled at her. "You love your coffee, don't you?"

Kirsty grinned, "I do. I can't wake up in the morning without it."

"Do you have a specific ritual in the morning?" Iain asked, surprised that they had never spoken about their morning routines. He hoped that the time would come soon that they could share it.

Kirsty's smile was sad as she said, "My grandfather and I used to have our first cup in the morning together. We then caught up with each other's news, talking about everything, except business. Those were our special times. These days I like to drink my first cup of coffee in the morning in silence. It is as if I still talk to my grandfather then."

"You miss him," Iain stated.

"I do," Kirsty admitted. "Since I was six, Joe had been my only family. He, and this place," Kirsty said, glancing around Joe's, "had been my one stability in life. About two weeks after I arrived to live with Joe, he brought me here. I was with him every step in making Joe's a reality. Even though I didn't understand what he was talking about, he spoke about it. You see those books?"

Iain nodded, and Kirsty said, "Most of them belonged to my parents. Others Joe and I chose over the years. Joe had only one rule. I first had to read the book before he allowed me to put it on the shelf," Kirsty smiled.

"Come," she said, inviting Iain to join her when she stood up, which he did in silence.

Kirsty stopped in front of the wall with photographs and pointed out one.

"This is your father and Joe with Joe's opening. There is Ellie, and her husband with Joe and this one is Major Maguire and Joe. These are my parents, and this is my grandmother. I never knew her. Oh, here is one of your mother and father with Joe taken long before Joe's opened, and this is your father and my Dad."

Iain had a lump in his throat when he stared at the photographs on the wall. He now understood Kirsty's statement that Joe's was her link to her grandfather. She must have had many memories locked up between these walls.

Iain took a deep breath before he went to stand behind Kirsty, wrapping his arms around her from behind. Now wasn't the time to tell her about his plans, but he knew he made the right decision. As Duncan had warned, Iain hoped keeping it as a surprise would not backfire. He didn't want to think about it now. He instead steered the conversation to happier memories for Kirsty. "Can you remember your first cup of coffee?"

Kirsty smiled, "My first taste of coffee and my first cup were two different occasions. My first taste was the day before Joe's opened. My grandfather and your father tested the coffee that day. They wanted to make sure everything was working as it should. They did it like everything else—with military preciseness," Kirsty chuckled. "Anyway, as they were drinking their coffee, I nagged my grandfather that I wanted coffee. He made me a cup of warm milk and added only a teaspoon of coffee in the milk. Over the years he added more teaspoons to my milk, and when I was thirteen, he brewed me my first cup. I was hooked."

Iain felt her relax against him, her head resting on his shoulder. Before he could react, Kirsty chuckled, "I don't have to ask you about your first cup of coffee."

Iain laughed, "No, I guess you don't, but as it was with you, I only had to taste it once, and I was hooked."

Kirsty leaned her head back to look at him, a mischievous smile curling on her lips, and Iain did what he had to do. He captured her mouth in a deep kiss, slipping his tongue inside and tasting the coffee she had a few minutes ago.

He hadn't lied. He only had to taste it once, and he was hooked, and it wasn't just the coffee.

That was also a discussion for another day. When he broke off the kiss, he nuzzled his nose in Kirsty's hair. Although he wanted to tell her how he felt, he wanted to do it properly. How he didn't know yet, but he knew it would not happen tonight.

When he felt more in control, he lifted his face and smiled down at her, "Why don't we go for a walk? It's not too cold yet."

"Hmm, I guess I need the fresh air. I spent all my time in Joe's the last few days while you were away. Where do you want to go?"

Iain checked his watch and said, "The Botanic Gardens will be open for another two hours if you want to go there. Inverleith is beautiful this time of the year, but it might be full of families. I need something more relaxing."

"Botanic Gardens it is. I haven't been there for a while."

It didn't take long for Kirsty to lock up or for them to drive the short distance to Inverleith Park. As Iain had predicted, there were several families in the park, enjoying the autumn day. He found a parking space in Inverleith Row near the

East Gate. The Gardens itself wasn't busy, and far more peaceful than the park.

On the southern boundary of the garden were trees that proved that autumn was with them. Shades of gold, yellow and orange, some even red, painted the lobed leaves of the trees.

The walk was everything Iain had hoped for. He could feel himself relax the further they walked. They talked about what had happened in the last few days and the plans for the next week. Iain enjoyed talking to Kirsty. He would love to discuss his business with her and would have liked her to do the same about Joe's. Every time he mentioned anything close to that, he could see Kirsty withdraw. It didn't look like she wanted him to know about her plans for Joe's, and Iain let it pass.

That evening they didn't want to go out. Iain was selfish, but he loved the time he could spend with her alone. In mutual agreement, they picked up a pizza on the way back from the gardens. Back at her apartment, they settled in front of the television, watching a movie. Actually, they didn't watch much of the film because Iain didn't miss the opportunity to cuddle up with Kirsty and steal a few kisses.

THE WEATHER DETERIORATED over the next few days. The need for jackets and scarves and gloves became necessary. Because of that, they didn't go out much that week and stayed in at Kirsty's apartment. Spending time in their cocoon meant more time for make-out sessions.

On Thursday night, Iain almost lost control. It started with a few sweet kisses, but it didn't stay like that, and somehow they ended up lying on her couch. Iain had looked down at Kirsty, and her hair spread over the arm of the sofa. Her lips were still swollen from their last kiss, and her eyes drowsy. She looked so beautiful that Iain couldn't help himself. He had to kiss her again. At first, the kiss was small, gentle and very meaningful, but it soon changed. It grew more intense, almost spiralling out of control.

Feeling her fingers tangling in his hair and her body arching into his, Iain knew he had to stop. How he had managed it, he didn't know. Even though he broke off the kiss, he didn't move away. He buried his face in her neck, breathing her in. He knew she could feel his erection brushing against her thigh. There was no way he could hide it from her.

It was time to take their relationship further. Kirsty's response had proved it.

SHE SHOULD HAVE KNOWN it would not stay the same forever. It might've felt like a high school love affair the way they behaved before. They kissed yes. They held hands, they cuddled, hugged and made out, but that was where it stayed. It was sweet but also frustrating. Now she knew. Iain was interested. His suit pants couldn't hide the evidence of his arousal.

Kirsty wondered about those moments in the past when Iain had pulled away from her in a hurry. She now knew that her thoughts that she wasn't good enough or that Iain didn't want her, was not the reason for his withdrawal from her.

Tonight he didn't pull away. Kirsty could feel his ragged breaths in her neck. His hand was shaking as he stroked it down her side. Hers was also shivering as she untangled them from his hair and brushed it over his back. She could still feel the effects of the kiss as she pressed closer to him.

When Iain lifted his head a long time later, they stared at each other. It was as if they communicated without words. When Iain spoke, at last, it sounded like a simple invitation, but Kirsty knew he implied so much more.

"Would you... Will you come with me to my house in Cramond on Saturday? Stay for dinner? And breakfast?"

Before Kirsty could answer, Iain shook his head, "No, don't answer now. Think about it and text me in the morning. You need to be sure."

Iain had left soon after, leaving Kirsty with her thoughts. She had thought about it throughout the night. Her body screamed to say yes. Her heart urged her to do so yet a bit of her mind warned her against it. It told her it would hurt when it was over.

She almost laughed at that. Yes, it would hurt, but it would hurt anyway. She already loved Iain too much not to hurt when things ended between them. The reality of life would soon hit them. Kirsty didn't want to think about it, but that was a fact.

All she needed to do was to prepare for when it would happen. So what should she do?

In the morning, she still had her doubts. Even her long and silent conversation with Joe hadn't helped to decide. She took a sip of her coffee and stared at her phone for a long time. Her fingers hovered over the send button.

When she pressed send, at last, she hoped she made the right decision.

"I won't join you for lunch on Sunday," Iain said when he put his phone down with a satisfied smile. When he looked up, he noticed that both his siblings were studying him.

"Oh, you have a hot date?" Graeme asked.

Iain flushed, which made Graeme and Aileen suspicious. Aileen exclaimed, "You have! Who is she? Is it someone we know?"

Iain glanced between the two before he admitted, "Yes. I might as well tell you as you'll soon find out anyway. It's Kirsty."

Aileen smiled, "You finally asked her out? It is about time, big brother."

Iain chuckled, "Not finally. We've been dating since July."

Aileen's mouth dropped open. Graeme blinked before he grinned, "Ah, now I understand where you disappeared to some weekends. I thought you spent time with Rab and Duncan."

Iain shook his head. "Kirsty and I have spent time with them over the last couple of weeks, but they were both away before."

Aileen asked with a curious expression, "So what makes this week special if you've already been dating for months?"

Iain nibbled on his bottom lip. Neither of his siblings sounded too surprised that he was seeing Kirsty. He wondered what they would think about his next step. "I'm taking her to the house."

Their eyes widened because they understood what Iain meant. He had made it clear after one disastrous relationship that he'd never take a woman home again if he were not serious about her. He hadn't in the eight years since then.

Graeme asked again, "You are serious about her?"

Iain nodded, "Yes, I am. Don't even say anything, because I know it may surprise or even shock you, but we haven't..."

Iain flushed because he knew he surprised his siblings, and himself that he hadn't taken Kirsty to his bed yet. Hell, not that he didn't want to, but with Kirsty... It was different. Special. He took a deep breath and admitted, "We haven't had sex yet. I want to take our relationship to the next level this weekend."

Ignoring his siblings' surprised—and amused faces, Iain instead shocked them more. "I want her to know what she's letting herself in for. After this weekend, she would have a better idea of who and what our family is. She's met you, and I had introduced her to Rab and Duncan who both liked her. I want to propose on Christmas Eve."

"Geez, Iain. I thought you would never settle, but I'm glad for you, Bro'. Anyway, I bet she's happy about her not having to move Joe's anymore," Graeme laughed.

Iain shook his head with a slight frown. He still had doubts about how to tell Kirsty of his plans for the building. Should he tell her now or keep it as a surprise?

Iain would have loved to have his father's advice. He glanced between his siblings. He wasn't sure how they would take this news, but since he couldn't ask his parents, his siblings might give him some clarity.

"I haven't told her yet. I wanted to keep it as a surprise, but I need to talk to her over the weekend. That is why I wanted to talk to you. I want to register Cairistìne Court in both my and Kirsty's names as a wedding present."

"Wow, that's big, Brother," Aileen exclaimed.

"I know, but it feels right, you know?" Iain tried to explain.

Aileen nodded, "Yeah, it does. You didn't want to believe me then, but I told you the similarity in the names is a sign. How do you feel about that, Graeme?"

Graeme studied Iain for so long that Iain didn't think his brother would agree. Graeme nodded, "If you feel it is the right thing to do."

"I do," Iain nodded. "I'm also getting Mum's rings cleaned. I thought I wanted to let you guys know."

It didn't surprise Kirsty when Iain walked into Joe's about an hour before closing time. She watched his progress as he walked towards the counter, exuding confidence. He slid into the chair right in front of her like he always did. He had confided some time ago to Kirsty that he was sitting there to be closer to her.

Though her staff had teased her from the beginning about Iain, Kirsty hadn't confided in anyone yet about what was between them. Why she didn't know, but it might be because she was not sure yet what it was. Yes, that might be it. They've never spoken about it since that first time. It was as if they fell into a relationship but never formalised it.

She knew her feelings and that she had seen no one else since they dated, but she didn't know about Iain. At this stage, she felt that if she didn't know about it, it didn't concern her.

Kirsty blushed bright red when Iain grinned, "Hey, Beautiful. Did you miss me?"

Her staff didn't miss that exchange. They couldn't miss Iain's frequent visits to Joe's or his outrageous flirting. That had escalated in the months since she went out with him the first time. She ignored the knowing look exchanged between her two best friends. They knew her well enough, and both Olivia and Morag had known about Kirsty's attraction.

By now, Iain had established that cappuccino was his favourite drink, so Kirsty didn't have to ask him anymore. She slid the cup over to him, and when he caught her fingers with his when he took the cup from her, Kirsty's breath hitched, and her eyes flew up to meet his. The smile tugged at the corner of his mouth when he whispered, "Ready?"

He didn't have to explain. Kirsty knew what he was asking but also knew he was giving her an out if she wanted to change her mind. She took a deep breath and nodded, "Yes."

His smile broadened, and he said nothing else. He leaned back in the chair and sipped his cappuccino as if he had no care in the world—which he probably didn't.

As it was Saturday, and most of the businesses in the vicinity had already closed, Joe's wasn't busy. The dreary weather also kept the tourists away, and for once, Kirsty closed earlier than usual. The staff cleaned the machines, and by two, they were ready to close for the day.

For the first time since they started dating, Iain waited for Kirsty. Most of the time, he either met her at her apartment or came to Joe's after hours, when the rest of the staff had already left.

Today, however, he took her weekend bag from her when she exited her office, making it clear to everyone he and Kirsty were leaving together. When she had finished locking up, Iain put his arm around her waist and led her to his car, waving to her staff as he helped her into the car.

Kirsty knew she could not avoid their questions on Monday.

9

Although Kirsty felt nervous about this next step in their relationship, she was also excited. Iain put her at ease, as he usually did, telling her about the house where he, and his father before him, grew up. His grandfather built the mansion just over eighty years ago. When they drove through the wooden gates with stone gate piers, something sparked a memory in Kirsty's mind. Iain drove down the tree- and shrub-lined drive that led to a vast gravel sweep in front of the house.

Iain drove past the panelled, painted hardwood front door to the back where the outbuildings housed the spacious garages. He apologised for taking her in through the back door, but Kirsty waved his apologies away.

Although the kitchen looked old-fashioned, it now boasted modern equipment and appliances. Whoever did it was smart, as it hadn't changed the ambience.

Iain took her on tour through the six-bedroomed house with its bright, spacious reception rooms. In common with the exterior, the interior of the house included many of the original features such as decorative cornices, hardwood floors and panelled walls, barrel-vaulted ceilings, operational shutters and original open fireplaces.

A wooden stairway led from the large inner hall to the first-floor landing, displaying carved balustrades. Four of the bedrooms were en-suite, and the other two shared the family bathroom. The original master bedroom looked old-fashioned, decorated with a massive four-poster bed. It was not Iain's style.

It didn't surprise Kirsty when he led her to a bedroom on the opposite side of the house with large windows on two fronts. Although it also had a large, king-size bed with a wooden headboard, the room was much lighter, with painted white walls and blue and maroon décor. A fireplace took up one wall with a comfortable leather couch in front. Above the fireplace, he mounted a massive, big-screen television on the wall. Books covered many of the flat spaces in the room. Kirsty smiled. This room reflected Iain's personality far more than the rest of the house.

Iain didn't linger in the room. He dropped her bag on the couch and took her hand to continue their tour. When Kirsty thought there was no more to see, Iain stopped in a smaller lounge downstairs where he lit the fire. While he did that, Kirsty surveyed the room.

The décor in this room was similar to Iain's bedroom, with big leather couches, a big-screen television, books, music system and fireplace. The décor differed from the rest of the house, so Kirsty surmised Iain had decorated these to his taste.

She stood at the window, taking in the lush gardens outside. Shrubs and trees lined the borders of the property, including beech, horse chestnut, oak and Scots pine. Iain came to stand behind her. He wrapped his arms around her middle and nuzzled her neck. Kirsty leaned back against him, enjoying his heat and strength. Iain lifted his head and brushed a kiss over her temple before he asked, "Fancy braving the cold to go for a tour of the garden? I believe the weather will get worse later on, and we might not get a chance."

Kirsty noticed the breeze had picked up. She was curious about the park-like garden and wondered if Iain and his siblings got up to any mischief there. She turned in his arms and smiled, "I'd love that."

They were so close she could see the darker blue rim accentuating his eyes. When he looked at her like he was now, Kirsty believed he cared. It was as if he only saw her, and she loved it. When he smiled, tiny crows feet appeared. He leaned in and brushed his mouth across hers. It was so brief, but it was enough to stoke anticipation of what was to come later. And it would. Kirsty knew it.

Iain stepped back and took her hand. In the little galley leading from the kitchen to the back door, he stopped to pull two outdoor jackets off the hooks. He wrapped Kirsty in one that smelled like him and was way too large for her. Again he gave her a brief kiss before he donned the other. He retook her hand and led her outside.

Iain's love for his childhood home was evident. He pointed out various corners of the garden where he and his siblings spent many hours. He pointed to one of the large oak trees, laughing, "See that tree? Rab, Duncan and I spent many hours in that tree with a book each, hiding from the younger two. Well, until the day Rab fell out of it and broke his arm. My Dad threatened to cut it down if we didn't stay out. By then, it didn't matter anymore. We've outgrown it."

"And your brother and sister never found out that is where you were hiding?" Kirsty asked with a laugh.

"No," Iain chuckled. "They still don't know that was where we were hiding."

As they walked through the garden with its well-kept lawn, Kirsty envied Iain his carefree upbringing. She was not complaining about hers, but it had been lonely, especially in the time before Olivia came to stay with Major Maguire, her great-uncle. Olivia had no other family when first her father got killed in Afghanistan, and then she had been removed from her mother's custody when she was fourteen. Maybe that was why Kirsty and Olivia had bonded. They each had to live with an elderly relative for much of their lives.

Peter was also an army brat. His father had been close friends with Joe, and Kirsty knew him for almost all her life. His mother was the mother that both she and Olivia needed during their teenage years. Having had only Peter, his mother loved mothering the two girls.

When Olivia went travelling, Kirsty had missed her. Now that Olivia was back, she wasn't the same. The pride and stubborn attitude hadn't changed, though. That was the girl Kirsty got to know. She only wished Olivia would accept her help. And she wished Olivia would confide in her on what happened when she returned to Scotland with a small baby, all alone. She hoped Olivia would tell in them one day.

Iain waved his hand in front of her face and asked, "Where did you go, Beautiful? You were far away."

Kirsty flushed, "Sorry, I was thinking about my childhood. I have to be honest, though. I envy you your childhood here. It must've been great having siblings around."

Iain nodded, "I guess. Don't tell them that, though. They had been real brats, but I love them. Yes, we had a great childhood growing up. It must've been different for you?"

Kirsty agreed, "I guess it was, and although I would have loved to have a sibling or two, I won't change the life I had with Joe for anything. He was not only my grandfather. He was my parent, my mentor and my confidante too. He had so much wisdom and knowledge and so many stories to tell. No child could be bored with Joe. And I had good friends like Livvie and Peter and now Morag too. Then there is Ellie and Major Maguire and some others who had passed away before Joe. We couldn't get into much mischief because they all kept an eye on us," she ended with a laugh.

As if in mutual agreement, they dropped the topic. For a while they walked in silence then Iain pointed to a stone cottage nestled in a quiet corner of the garden, "You've met David. That is where he and his wife, Chrissie lives. Chrissie makes sure I don't starve and that I don't drown under dust and dirty dishes. They'd been here forever."

Around the corner from the first cottage was another, built in the same style as the first. "That is where the groundsman and his wife live. They are a younger couple and take care of the gardens and help with maintenance around the property."

Kirsty laughed, "I don't envy them their jobs. This place is like a park."

"It is, isn't it? Before my grandfather bought this place, it was farmland around here. The village expanded over the years and now the property is on the outskirts. I still think it is too big, but there is nothing I can do about it. The house and the land are locked in trust."

"Isn't it lonely living here alone?" Kirsty asked when they made their way back to the house.

Iain gave her an intense look. It looked like he wanted to say something, but then he stopped himself. He waited until they were inside and helped her to take off his jacket. He hung the coats up and then turned to her, pulling her into his arms. With his chin resting on her hair, he whispered, "It is lonely now, but I hope not for much longer. Soon I would like to have my wife, and children to share it with me."

Kirsty had to swallow hard, glad he couldn't see how much that was hurting. He didn't have to tell her that when he makes his choice for a future wife, the mother of his children, she would no longer be part of his life.

Being here at the house where he grew up, Kirsty came to realise how different their worlds were. She had no expectations about the relationship lasting.

Iain closed his eyes, willing himself to take it slow. He had been so close to telling Kirsty how he felt. It felt so right having her here with him, showing her what he hoped would be her future home and a place where they could raise their children, just as his parents had raised them.

He loved Logan's Walk, the house where he and his siblings had grown up, and he hoped that Kirsty would come to love it too. Iain would give her free rein in modernising the furniture to their tastes.

In the kitchen, he stopped to open a bottle of her favourite red wine. With the bottle and two glasses in hand, he led Kirsty to the small lounge where he lit the fire earlier. They cuddled on the couch in front of the fireplace that had now warmed up the room. The firelight bathed the room in soft light, making it cosy and intimate.

Darkness settled and here, so close to the sea, the wind had picked up. The rain was steadily beating against the window, but Iain and Kirsty didn't feel the cold, cuddling so close. As usual, the conversation between them flowed, but they would often sit in silence, feeling comfortable with each other. When Kirsty's tummy rumbled, Iain laughed, and Kirsty flushed. Iain got up, pulling Kirsty with him. "We don't have to cook. Knowing Chrissie, she would have stocked the freezer and the fridge with homemade meals. She and David went to visit their children near Inverness, and she thinks I would starve if she's not here to take care of me."

"Well," Kirsty teased, "I've seen evidence of your cooking skills…"

Iain's mouth dropped open in mock consternation, "How dare you criticise my cooking? Wait until I get hold of you."

He lunged toward her. Kirsty shrieked, and with a laugh, she jumped out of his reach before she took off. Iain stood still, completely taken by surprise. This was a different side of Kirsty she didn't show often. He must admit that he loved it.

Without a thought, he chased her and caught up with her before she reached the kitchen. His arm slipped around her middle, and he pulled her back against him with one arm. The other pressed in her neck where he had found out by accident she was ticklish. She giggled and tried to get away, but Iain was relentless.

When she lay limp from laughter against him, Iain stopped his onslaught. He pressed his mouth in her neck and kissed the spot he so recently tickled. With a small sigh, Kirsty relaxed and lifted her face to give him better access.

Iain trailed his mouth over her jaw, and with his hand, he turned her face towards him. Their mouths met in a sweet, sweet kiss, filling Iain's soul.

The tiny little doubt that had still lingered in his mind disappeared. This was it. She was it. She was the woman who completed his soul.

When he lifted his mouth, they stared at each other in wonder and then they both smiled.

He let her go to rummage for food. That kiss was enough for now. It wouldn't be enough later.

DINNER WAS a thick broth and freshly baked bread. Iain only needed to warm it up, which didn't take long. They had their meal sitting on the thick carpet with their bowls on the coffee table.

After dinner, while Kirsty put their dinner things away, Iain had slipped up the stairs to light the fire in his room. Downstairs, he pushed the coffee table away from the couch. He had just added more logs to the fire when Kirsty entered the room with another glass of wine for each of them.

He had pulled pillows from the couch and settled his back against it. Kirsty nestled against him and in perfect harmony, they enjoyed their wine and talked. When they finished their wine, Iain put their glasses on the coffee table, and they settled back, still talking, but for the last few minutes, their conversation had ceased.

Iain could feel the electricity, the anticipation building in the room, and he took a deep breath. He grazed his hand up and down Kirsty's back, feeling the heat of her body where she lay huddled against his chest. He felt her hand rub his chest, down to his stomach, and he shivered.

Kirsty lifted her head from his shoulder, turning to look at him. When her hand slid under his shirt, rubbing the naked skin underneath, Iain groaned. His hand tangled in her hair and took her mouth in a long and slow kiss. Her hand caressing his skin became bolder, and Iain broke the kiss with shuddering breaths. He grabbed the shirt at the back of his neck and pulled it over his head. Kirsty helped him to tear it down his arms and threw it on the couch behind him. Her hands started their exploration again, leaving Iain weak-kneed.

Iain pulled her on top of him so she could straddle him and claimed her mouth. His hands tightened against her hips, but then he, just as eagerly as Kirsty, started his own exploration. His hands slid under her thin sweater, lifting it with each stroke. He only broke the kiss to pull her shirt over her head. He let her lean back a little so his eyes could feast on her creamy skin, the firm swell of her breasts of which the pink nipples taunted him through the white lace of her bra.

"You're so beautiful," he managed while his hands lifted to her breasts, stroking her through her bra. Kirsty moaned and wiggled over him. Iain groaned with her. His hands shook when he tried to find the catch of her bra, asking through gritted teeth, "unfasten your hair, please? I would like to see how it looks against your skin."

Kirsty smiled a little, holding his eyes when she lifted her hands to the plait and removed the elastic. She let it drop to the floor and used her fingers to free the three separate strings and comb it through.

Iain unfastened the clasp of her bra, pushing it off her shoulders at the same time her hair tumbled over her shoulders in one glorious mass. Iain stared at the vision in front of him. She was gold and fire, and she heated him in places no other woman had ever done before.

His hands trembled when he lifted them to her, stroking the hair away from her shoulders. His fingers stroke, almost reverently to the top of her breasts, but then his hands got greedy. He wanted to feel her in his palms, and he cupped her. He watched fascinated as the nipple hardened under the brushing of his thumb.

He needed just one kiss, one taste.

He pulled her up, and then his tongue tasted her at last. Soft, sweet, like honey with an added aroma of vanilla. Her moans drove him crazy, and his mouth closed over one nipple, sucking it in his mouth. His one hand caressed her other breast, and the other explored the rest of the soft skin exposed to his hands.

Iain wanted more. His mouth left her breast, trailing wet kisses up, over her chest, and collarbone, her neck and at last, his lips claimed hers. He pulled her tight against him with one arm and the other tangled in her hair, deepening the kiss.

Kirsty moved against him, rubbing her breasts against his chest, causing unbearable friction.

Iain couldn't remember how things progressed from there. Somehow, in a matter of minutes, they got rid of the rest of their clothes. Their movements had become more urgent while they discovered each other with touch and taste.

Iain still couldn't get over how beautiful Kirsty had looked, the firelight bathing her skin, her smile, her tangled hair and the golden-brown eyes staring into his when he entered her the first time. That memory, their fingers tangled on each side of her head, would stay forever in his mind. When they lay spent in each other's arms, their breathing laboured, Iain took a shuddering breath.

"I promise next time I'll have more control and take it slow, *mo leannan.*"

He heard Kirsty's low chuckle against his ear, "Are you sure about that?"

Iain lifted his head, looking at her. He noticed the small smile at the corners of her mouth, and he smiled back.

"I swear I used to have control. Hell, how I managed the last few months, I don't know but now, with you... If it is like this every time, *mo leannan*, I would not have a shred of control left."

"Mo leannan? That's Gaelic. What does that mean?" Kirsty asked.

Iain smiled, "I think it means sweetheart or something. But don't expect more Gaelic from me. That's the extent of my vocabulary. I only know that one because it was what my grandfather called my grandmother. He was from Skye and still spoke Gaelic."

Kirsty smiled, "I like that."

Iain leaned over, claiming her mouth in a slow and gentle kiss. He pulled the afghan from the couch, settled pillows behind his head and pulled Kirsty against his chest. For a long time, they lay like that, talking until they both drifted off to sleep.

Much later in the night, Iain banked the fire and folded the afghan around Kirsty. He picked the sleepy woman up in his arms and carried her to his bedroom. Iain settled her in his bed, watching how she huddled underneath the blanket. With a smile went to the bathroom. When he came back, he slipped under the sheets, spooning Kirsty from behind and soon fell asleep.

He woke up the next morning with Kirsty trailing kisses over his chin, his cheeks and down to his chest. Iain chuckled, "Good morning," and he swiftly turned her on her back, claiming her mouth.

Their lovemaking was more relaxed than the previous night, but it was no less passionate.

Iain wasn't surprised when it was already almost eleven when they got dressed. He needed to remember that if he ever was in a hurry, he shouldn't share a shower with Kirsty. She was too much of a distraction. Not that he complained about it.

10

The weather had cleared a little although rain was in the forecast for later that afternoon. Iain convinced Kirsty that they needed food and fresh air, and if she went for a walk on the beach with him, he would take her out to lunch. Their walk didn't last long, as the wind had picked up, and when they arrived at Iain's favourite pub in South Queensferry, the sky was overcast again.

Fraser's was a typical Scottish country pub with a rustic character. It had a similar atmosphere as Joe's, and Kirsty loved it.

The staff and patrons knew Iain well because, as he explained to Kirsty, they often came here for Sunday lunch as did most of the other regulars. They used to do it with his grandparents, then with his dad and recently the three siblings had picked up the tradition again.

As they made their way to a table in the corner, some regulars stopped Iain. Kirsty noticed the curious glances of the women. When an elderly occupant of another table stopped them, Kirsty couldn't miss the open hostility of one woman. It was quite a large table, and Iain only introduced her as Kirsty. He had put his arm around Kirsty's waist and pulled her against him. To anyone in the pub, they would look like a loving couple.

An older man who sat two seats from the hostile woman, beamed at Kirsty, "You are Joe's little girl, aren't you?"

Kirsty's eyes widened. "Yes. Did you know my grandfather?"

"Yes," the older man laughed, "he was my commander in the army. I was in the same regiment as this boy's father," he added, gesturing to Iain.

He sobered up. "I'm sorry. You both had suffered a loss this last year, but it's good you are together. Your father and grandfather would have liked that. Every time they got together they bragged about you, lamenting you've never met."

"Us?" Kirsty and Iain asked simultaneously. She could feel Iain squeezing her waist when the older man nodded.

"Yes, they've been scheming for years to get you together."

Kirsty looked up at Iain, noticing the smile on his face and then, something flashed in his eyes before he bent down and pecked her on the forehead. She was glad for his arm around her because she wasn't sure what she read in his eyes. Whatever it was, made her legs feel weak.

Iain excused them. Nobody stopped them again until they reached their table. Thank goodness for that. She needed to sit. She still felt as if she couldn't breathe properly after that moment they shared.

The table to which the waitress led them was big enough for four. To Kirsty's surprise, Iain didn't sit opposite her. Instead, he slid into the bench next to her and flung his arm around her shoulder.

She had a brief thought that it looked like he wanted to give someone a message. Kirsty had an uncomfortable feeling it might be the woman who still shot daggers in her direction. Iain, however, seemed oblivious. He hadn't even looked at the woman or acknowledged her. As usual, it felt to Kirsty as if he focused all his attention on her, Kirsty.

They ordered a glass of wine each, and a Sunday roast platter for two. According to Iain, the pub was famous for its Sunday lunch specials. Roast beef and slow-cooked short rib of beef and gravy served with roast potatoes, roast carrots, parsnips and Yorkshire pudding, filled the plate. Although the food was delicious, Kirsty couldn't eat half of the food on her plate, but Iain didn't have that problem. When Kirsty commented on it, he wiggled his eyebrows at her, saying, "I worked up quite an appetite, Sweetheart."

Kirsty flushed, which caused Iain to chuckle. He leaned in and kissed her. His eyes had darkened when he lifted his mouth. He studied her face, then pleaded, "Stay with me tonight? I'm not ready to let you go."

Kirsty studied his face, saw the sincerity in his eyes and nodded her agreement. She anyway wasn't ready to end their time. Iain captured her mouth in a slow kiss, oblivious to the people around them.

They both jumped when a hand slapped on the table, and someone said, "Get a room, you two."

Iain growled, "Go away," but he pulled away reluctantly to glare at Graeme and Aileen.

The newcomers ignored Iain's grumpiness and pulled out chairs, making themselves at home at the table. Graeme smirked, "It's the weekend. You're not our boss now and anyway it's a free country. This is our usual table."

Iain growled at him and slapped Aileen's hand when she tried to sneak one of the roast potatoes left on the platter. "It is, but it's our date and our lunch."

His younger brother and sister looked at each other, shook their heads and smiled at their older brother. Graeme waved to the waitress who knew the three Young siblings and their preferences. She soon came back with a glass of wine for Aileen and a beer on tap for Graeme.

Iain exhaled, and Kirsty laughed. She never had brothers and sisters, but even though Iain looked exasperated, she could see that the three enjoyed each other's company. She patted Iain's hand, saying, "They don't bother me, Iain. Let them stay."

Aileen beamed at her. "I knew I liked you, Kirsty. See, big brother, your girlfriend doesn't mind us, so you can't say anything."

She held up her glass of wine to Kirsty and smiled, ignoring Kirsty's flushed face. "To new friendships."

To which Iain groaned, "We should have stayed at home, *mo leannan*. I could have had you all to myself then."

Kirsty didn't miss the look Iain's siblings shared when they heard the endearment. Neither commented on it, sparing Kirsty more blushes.

It surprised her that she relaxed and had an enjoyable afternoon. She had met both Aileen and Graeme before, but it was the first time since she and Iain had seen each other that they spent time together.

Iain must have said something to them because neither of them had looked surprised to see Kirsty. Aileen, in particular, was good company and filled Kirsty in on the gossip on the other patrons in the pub. When her eyes fell on the woman Kirsty had noticed earlier, she bumped Graeme's arm.

"Oh look, there's the Piranha."

Graeme and Iain admonished her, but Aileen confided in Kirsty, "She is one. She only chases after rich men and has been trying for years with Iain. Luckily he never gave her the time of day. I shudder to think if she had to be my sister-in-law. Thank goodness that will never happen now. You should be careful, Brother," she added, bumping Graeme's arm. "She may now aim her charms at you."

Graeme snorted.

"You want more wine, Aileen?" Iain asked clipped, narrowing his eyes at his sister. Aileen studied him for a moment and probably read something in Iain's face because she kept quiet. She shrugged, taking a sip of her wine.

After that exchange, Iain didn't want to stay longer. He settled their bill, said goodbye to his siblings and took Kirsty's hand, leading her out of the bar. The walk back to his house didn't take long.

Iain lit the fire in the bedroom, and the rest of the afternoon, they spent making love and watching old movies and talking. Later that night, after they had a dinner of wine, biscuits and cheese while cuddling on the couch in his room, Iain asked Kirsty, "I'm curious. What was the relationship between my father and your grandfather?"

Kirsty turned her head and asked, surprised, "You don't know?"

Iain shook his head, "No, the first time I heard about their friendship was just before you and I met."

Kirsty took a sip of her wine before she answered, "I don't know the whole story, as my grandfather was always reluctant to talk about it. All I know is that my grandfather saved your father's life during the Falkland War."

"From that photographs in Joe's I gathered they knew each other for a long time," Iain surmised.

"Yes, they did. I don't know if you know that your parents were my godparents. I've been here, in this house, when I was about four but that's all I can remember. It was just before we went to South Africa. My grandfather told me years later that your father paid for my father's studies, and my father wanted to tell him the good news about the contract he got. That's why we were here. I know your father also helped my grandfather after my parents died to bring their bodies, and me, back to Scotland. My grandfather had left the army then and started Joe's."

Iain frowned, "I've wondered about it since I've heard about the building. Why have we never met you or Joe or heard of that building? It was as if my father kept that part of his life away from us."

Kirsty flushed, remembering her conversation with her grandfather. The Young siblings were as much in the dark as she was.

Iain studied her face and asked, "Is there something you're not telling me?"

Kirsty grimaced, but then told him about that conversation with her grandfather when she accused Drew of being ashamed of them.

Iain pulled her into his arms, rubbing his hands over her back and kissing her hair. He mused, "Hm, that's possible. My dad never spoke about his time in the army. We've seen photos of him in uniform, but he always changed the subject when we asked him about it."

Kirsty nestled in his arms, feeling safe and protected for the first time in a long time. They didn't speak again about their families. As if in mutual agreement, they didn't speak at all. Iain picked Kirsty up and carried her to the bed where he joined her. Their lovemaking was tender, and they fell asleep in each other's arms.

Iain pushed his hands through his hair in frustration. He turned to glare at Moira. "Do I have to go tomorrow?"

Moira replied, "You know you don't have a choice, Iain. Your father always attended. Be there. It's not every day you get nominated for the Young Businessman of the Year Award."

"That's stupid. All I did was sell half the company my father built up. I did nothing special," Iain grumbled.

Moira's look was enough to stop Iain from grumbling any further. They had this discussion a few times over the last few weeks. He should know better than to argue with her.

"Can Kirsty go with me?" Iain tried again.

"No, unfortunately not. We've been through this how many times. It is invitation only, and you only got an invitation for yourself, the same as your siblings. If you'd asked me before, we might have used Aileen's invitation, but she had already declined."

Iain sighed resignedly, "Okay. I'll go. You know what to do, but I have one stipulation though. I'm only staying tomorrow night. I don't want to hang around in London. Get the earliest flight back on Saturday morning."

"What about the interview with *Business Today?* When should we schedule it?"

Iain frowned. He would have liked to have the interview before the Business Circle Dinner, but because of the nomination, it might be better to do it afterwards. He said to Moira, "Arrange an early breakfast meeting for Saturday morning. Arrange my return flight for around mid-morning."

Moira didn't answer, but she got busy while Iain walked into his office. His phone vibrated in his pocket, and he took it out. When he saw the caller ID, Iain declined the call. He wasn't in the mood today for his ex. He had enough to deal with, but maybe he should see her while he was in London and clarify that he wasn't interested. Well, he had made it clear before he left London, but she didn't want to take no for an answer.

Since the article had appeared in the papers earlier this week about his nomination for the Young Businessman of the Year Award, Lydia had phoned him. The first couple of times, Iain had made the mistake of answering, but now he declined her calls. He guessed that was another reason he didn't look forward to going to this awards thing without Kirsty.

He was ready to take the next step with Kirsty, but the timing was out. He wanted to be here with Kirsty as Iain knew that it was difficult for her. He had seen how quiet she became since the first tenants moved out of Cairistìne Court the last couple of weeks. The only remaining tenant would vacate the premises on Friday, just when he had to be in London.

Maybe he should have spoken to Kirsty about his ideas for the building, but Iain wanted to surprise her. His plans were in place. He had promised the construction crew a big bonus if they worked on Sunday. It was Kirsty's weekend off, and Iain's only job would be to keep her away from Joe's. On Sunday, the crew would take off the old sign, clean the wall and put up the new sign Iain had made. The new sign would only read, Cairistìne Court, as it was before, but underneath it would be another sign with the names of the only other tenants in the building—Young's and just below it, Joe's Coffee House.

Iain had even planned a small ceremony with his siblings, Moira and Kirsty present. Kirsty, although she didn't know it yet, would be the one to do the revealing.

It was only a few more days, Iain encouraged himself. He needed to keep it a secret until Monday at the latest.

Iain sighed. It was no use thinking about that now. He picked up the first folder in front of him, and soon Iain immersed himself in business. He finished with the documentation on his desk just before six. He took out his phone to text David that he was ready to leave. He tried to be home before Kirsty as he wanted to treat her tonight.

The building was quiet when Iain got in the lift to take him down to the basement area where David was waiting. On their way to Leith, Iain gave David instructions. He would stay with Kirsty tonight but would stop at home tomorrow to pick up his tuxedo on the way to the airport.

Kirsty wasn't in yet when Iain arrived at her apartment. She had given him a key after the first weekend she had stayed at his house, and Iain let himself in.

It had become a routine that Iain would stay a couple of nights a week with Kirsty in town. Weekends, after Kirsty had closed up, she would remain with Iain in Cramond.

Although it was still supposed to be autumn, the last couple of days had been wet and cold, so Iain adjusted the old thermostat. Kirsty had been complaining about it being temperamental, and although Iain itched to get it fixed, he had learned that Kirsty would not like his interference. He hadn't earned that right yet, but Iain hoped it would be soon.

Iain already felt that Christmas Eve was too far away. He was ready to take the next step, but was Kirsty?

He took off his jacket and pulled off his tie before he rolled up his sleeves. He set the oven to warm up the lasagne and garlic bread David had brought from home. Iain had already set the table when he got Kirsty's message she was on the way. Iain opened a bottle of wine and then ran a bath for Kirsty before he went back to the kitchen to finish his dinner preparations. Iain was busy making a salad when he heard Kirsty's key in the door. She looked tired when she walked into the kitchen, a wan smile on her face.

"It smells nice in here," she said and leaned in to kiss him.

"Hey, Beautiful. You look tired. Did you have a busy day?" Iain asked when Kirsty pulled away.

Kirsty exhaled, "Yes! I don't think I've sat down for a moment. It felt as if the whole population of Edinburgh was in Joe's today."

Iain finished the salad and put it to the side. He wiped his hands on the cloth he had tucked in his belt and then poured Kirsty a glass of wine with instructions.

"There's a warm bath waiting for you. Relax while I finish up here."

Kirsty smiled and kissed Iain again. She took a sip of her wine and said over her shoulder, "A girl can get used to this."

She had disappeared by the time Iain murmured, "That's what I'm bargaining on, my Love," but Iain didn't think she heard.

Much later that evening, after they had dinner and were cuddling with a mug of hot chocolate on the couch, Iain reluctantly mentioned, "I won't be here tomorrow night. I have to go to London, but I'll be back on Saturday. Do you have any plans for the weekend?"

Kirsty frowned and then she said, "No, nothing specific. I work Saturday though."

"I'll be back around lunchtime on Saturday. Do you want to go to Cramond for the weekend?"

Kirsty stayed quiet for a while which had Iain worried. Was she pulling back? Was he moving too fast? He almost sighed with relief when she agreed, "Yeah, okay."

Before Iain could say anything, his phone rang. He picked it up, saw it was Lydia again and declined the call. He put the phone back on the table next to him and pulled Kirsty back against his chest.

They sat in silence, watching Iain's favourite detective series, although Iain wasn't concentrating on it. He had a feeling something was wrong, and he didn't know what. Before he could broach the delicate subject, he heard Kirsty's even breathing and knew she was asleep.

He didn't know what was wrong, and he would have liked to fix it tonight. Now it would not happen.

Iain moved, stood up and then picked Kirsty up. She didn't even stir when he lay her gently on the bed and covered her with the duvet. Iain returned to the lounge and picked up their discarded cups. He took it to the kitchen and cleaned up, deep in thought.

By the time Iain had finished putting everything away and joined Kirsty in bed, he already concluded that he had only one option. It scared the hell out of him that he was making the wrong decision, but he had no choice. He had to do it, even though it might be the most challenging thing he ever had to do.

11

Kirsty woke up early, long before her alarm clock woke her. She felt disoriented wondering how she got in bed because she couldn't remember getting into it. She didn't have to wonder about it too long, because she felt Iain's arm tightening around her. His hand moved, slipping under the loose T-shirt she had put on last night after her bath.

She smiled, arching her back against him. She didn't have to wonder where this was going because she could feel his arousal against her leg. Kirsty moved away and turned to him. Iain didn't hesitate. His mouth claimed hers, the kiss hungry and sensual. His lovemaking was just as intense, and to Kirsty, it almost felt desperate. It didn't take them long to reach that moment where it felt as if the world exploded around them. Afterwards, they lay spent in each other's arms. Kirsty didn't know how long they cuddled there, without talking, before Iain lifted his head from her shoulder and smiled, "Good morning, Beautiful."

Kirsty smiled, stroking his hair from his forehead, "Good morning, Handsome."

Iain exhaled, and then he rolled over, pulling Kirsty with him. His arms encircled her, keeping her close. Kirsty heard his murmur, "I need to leave earlier today. I have a lot to do before my flight, but I need to hold you for a while."

Kirsty didn't answer. She didn't know what to say because something felt different this morning.

No, Iain was different. The way he held her, the way he had kissed her and the way they had made love almost felt desperate. Kirsty slipped her arms around his waist and lay still, holding him as tight as he was holding her.

After a long time, Iain sighed, "I need to get going."

His arms loosened its grip on her. Kirsty felt the gentle kiss on her hair, and then he slipped out of bed. He didn't look at her again before he disappeared from the room towards the bathroom.

Kirsty heard the shower and got up. She shivered as the cold morning air hit her skin and got dressed in a warm sweater and tracksuit pants. She would shower and get dressed later when Iain had left.

Kirsty pulled on warm socks and made her way to the kitchen to make coffee. The percolator had just run when Iain's phone rang. He must have plugged it into the charger in the kitchen last night, as he did when he stayed here.

Kirsty worried that it might be important because it was so early and picked up the phone. She was just too late as it went to voice-mail before she could answer. Kirsty glanced at the screen, noticing that there were several missed calls from one of his contacts, Lydia, but then a message came in from the same person.

Kirsty only read, "See you tonight. I miss...," but then the screen shut off.

Kirsty put the phone down and turned away to pour herself a cup of coffee. She leaned against the counter, cuddling the mug in both hands, deep in thought.

That was how Iain found her a short while later. As she didn't acknowledge him, Iain didn't speak. He poured himself a mug, taking a sip. Kirsty watched while Iain picked up his phone. He studied the screen, probably noticing the missed calls and the message and then he glanced at her.

To Kirsty's already suspicious mind, he almost looked guilty, but he said nothing. Iain finished his coffee, a frown marring his forehead.

He rinsed the mug and left it on the drying rack before he turned towards Kirsty. He studied her face for a long time. With a soft sigh, he cupped her face in his hands and murmured, "We need to talk when I come back."

Kirsty didn't have time to answer, as Iain kissed her, long and deep. She hated her automatic response to the kiss, but then she realised that this might be the last time, and she kissed him back. Eventually, he pulled away. It looked like he wanted to say something, but then he stepped back. His last words, just before he disappeared through the door with his overnight bag were, "See you."

. . .

"See you," Kirsty fumed, sliding her gaze between her two friends. "What did that mean? Was that how you say goodbye to the woman with whom you just had sex? See you! That almost felt like an insult."

Olivia snorted, "At least you got a 'see you'."

Kirsty's heart clenched. Was that happening with her and Iain? She looked up when Morag sympathised, "I know it upsets you because all the tenants are now out of the building. Don't you think you're blowing this out of proportion?"

Kirsty thought about it. Hell, all she did the whole day was think about what happened this morning. Morag had seen she was upset and that was the reason for this impromptu girls' night at Olivia's apartment.

No, this was not her imagination. Things were different with Iain last night and this morning. She remembered the desperation in his lovemaking. She shook her head, "No, I don't think so. I haven't told you, but this morning, while Iain was in the shower, he got a phone call."

"And?" Olivia urged.

Kirsty told them what happened the previous night when Iain also got a phone call and he declined it. He had the same guilty expression this morning when he checked his phone and saw the missed calls and messages.

"That means nothing, Kirsty," Morag pointed out.

"I know, but I feel... After Iain checked his phone, he told me we need to talk when he comes back. Maybe he wants to end it?" Kirsty mumbled.

"Don't jump to conclusions," Morag warned.

"I know, I know. As I've said, maybe I feel unsettled now that the last tenants moved out. In all these months Iain and I haven't once spoken about Joe's moving. It's as if we both avoided the topic, so I still don't know what he's planning to do. But, I have a surprise for him. The building can stand empty, but I'm not moving. I owe it to Drew and my grandfather."

Olivia frowned, "What do you mean?"

"I'm sorry. I know I didn't tell you that Iain wanted me to move Joe's so he can sell the building or something. You've been going through a rough patch with Matti and your work. I can't let it happen. That building meant so much to Drew. I can't let him tear it down!"

Kirsty looked at Olivia when she was looking uncomfortable, "You've been working at Young's. Haven't you heard anything?"

Olivia shook her head, "Kirsty, you can't ask me that."

Kirsty sighed, "I know. I'm not fair."

She stood up, putting her empty glass on the counter, "I'm going home. I'll deal with everything tomorrow."

Both her friends got up while Kirsty ordered a cab. Outside she shivered when the cold breeze hit her face. She huddled deeper in her jacket as the taxi pulled up in front of the building.

The unsettled feeling hadn't left yet when she entered her apartment. The silence awaiting her added to her gloomy mood.

She didn't sleep well and was up early on Saturday morning. Instead of waiting at home for the time to pass, Kirsty went to Joe's early. She had paperwork to do that might keep her mind off the nagging feeling that something was wrong.

She let herself into Joe's long before the usual opening time. Kirsty switched on the lights and started her preparations for the day. First, she adjusted the heating to combat the chill in the air before she switched on the coffee machine to heat. She worked almost on autopilot when she filled the hopper with fresh beans and pulled an espresso to test the grind. Soon the smell of ground and brewed coffee filled the air.

A long time ago, Joe had given up roasting their coffee. He had tried at first, but as the business in Joe's increased, Joe felt he couldn't provide his clients with the quality he needed. Since then they had bought their coffee and teas from a master roaster in Portobello where Kirsty had also done her training. She still visited the merchant regularly to refresh her training and find out about the new products the company has.

She sat in Iain's usual chair and enjoyed her first cup of the day. Other days the silence in Joe's and the aroma of the coffee would help her relax, but not today. The miserable feeling she had since yesterday still hadn't left.

She struggled to get past the heaviness in her chest. She tried to discuss her dilemma with Joe, as she always did. Today she missed her grandfather more than ever. She wished he was there to give her advice. She could almost hear him, remembering his advice after she parted ways with Lachlan Thompson.

"Sometimes you got to wise up and let go. It may hurt now, but it will hurt even more in the future."

He had been right. Lachlan was a fake and had used Kirsty to impress Drew Young. Of course, it didn't work. Although Drew and her grandfather arranged a blind date for them neither had been a big fan of him when it finished. Lachlan cheated on her, and when Kirsty confronted him, he told her she was just a way to get to Drew. Lachlan had not been the first though. Maybe that was why she was so wary of getting involved with Iain. He came from the same background as Lachlan.

Until now, she thought he was different.

What advice would Joe have given her today? That she was a fool for hoping Iain would commit? No, maybe he would have used some of his other words of wisdom he had picked up over the years. Kirsty had often heard him say to the young baristas when they were heartbroken over a failed relationship: *Just because a person is right for you, you may not be the right one for them.*

That might be closer to the truth. Kirsty had known that from the beginning. They've never been poor because Joe was too cunning for that. Her grandmother was a doctor in the army. Joe had invested her pension and also those of Kirsty's parents' insurance money, but she'll never be in Iain's league. Not that she wanted to be. Her life was here with Joe's. Apart from having her own family one day, Joe's was all she wanted or needed.

That was until Iain.

She had put aside her wariness of getting involved with Iain over the last few weeks since they became lovers. She had let what was between her and Iain lull her into some kind of domestic bliss. She had hoped for a Happy Ever After, but she had to face reality. The sooner she did that, the better.

Kirsty poured another cup of coffee and opened her laptop to finish the orders for the next week. She only looked up when she heard a rap on the door. She smiled when she saw the young boy who delivered the papers on the weekends. Kirsty poured him a cup of coffee in a takeaway cup and went to open the door. While they exchanged greetings, Kirsty traded the stack of papers for the coffee.

When the boy was on his way, she finished the orders and got Joe's ready for the first customers. When she finished checking that everything was clean and the machines in the kitchen were warming up, she took out the papers from its plastic wrapping and sorted them out.

A photograph on the Scottish Daily caught her eye, and Kirsty stopped. She read the article accompanying the picture almost three times before it sank in. The first time her hand shook too much, and her brain felt numb.

Kirsty concentrated on the paper and didn't hear Morag and Peter's arrival. When she felt a hand on her shoulder, Kirsty looked up, oblivious to the tears in her eyes.

Morag didn't need to ask what was going on, because her eyes had fallen on the paper Kirsty still clutched in her hand. Morag took the now crumpled paper from Kirsty. She heard Peter's curses while he and Morag read the article. Kirsty heard them talking, and then she felt Morag's hand on her arm.

"You should go home, Kirsty. You can't work today."

Kirsty shook her head and looked at them. "I don't want to be alone."

Peter shook his head, "You don't have to be. Morag and I had just discussed it. I'm taking you to Ellie's."

Kirsty closed her eyes and nodded, "Yes. Yes, of course. Thank you."

IAIN SANK into his seat with a sigh, grateful that it was over, and he had boarded the plane without a newshound in sight. Last night, after the awards ceremony, he did the interview scheduled for this morning and changed his flight to the first one leaving Heathrow. Afterwards, Iain celebrated with Graeme, much later and much harder than he had planned to do. He remembered he had confided in Graeme what he had planned for tonight. Even though Graeme agreed that it might backfire, he supported Iain's decision.

Iain felt tired and bleary-eyed because when he fell into bed in the early hours of the morning, he couldn't sleep. Iain guessed his mind was on what he needed to do today. He was still worried. He could only hope he was doing the right thing.

He lifted his hand and massaged his neck. It felt stiff, just as his shoulders. He tried to roll them, but it didn't bring much relief. Iain closed his eyes and leaned back against the seat.

He felt, rather than saw someone taking the seat next to him, but he wasn't ready for small talk. His fellow passenger had other ideas because he bumped Iain's arm and chuckled "Rough night?"

Iain opened his eyes with a sigh and frowned. "What are you doing here? I thought you're staying for the weekend."

"Change of plans, Bro'," Graeme grinned, "Same as you. Would you mind if David drops me at my house?"

Iain shook his head, "No, as long as he drops me off first. I want to crash for an hour or so before I pick up Kirsty."

Graeme snorted. "You look like you need it. Did you party after you left me?"

"No, I went to bed, but I struggled to sleep. I had had too much to drink," Iain snorted. "I'm getting too old for this."

"Yes, you're almost ancient," Graeme agreed. Iain didn't have the energy to bite, but Graeme only pretended to feel better than Iain because he also stayed quiet. The stewardess woke Iain a short while later. It didn't surprise Iain to see Graeme also wiping his eyes as if he had just woken up.

Iain texted David as soon as they entered the airport building. The airport was still quiet, and they didn't have to wait long for their luggage that early in the morning. David was waiting at his usual spot. Iain and Graeme both greeted the older man, and he only grunted a greeting at Iain. Iain frowned, as it was unusual behaviour for David. He spoke to Graeme, however, and ignored Iain for the rest of the way to Cramond.

Iain frowned, but he said nothing. It surprised him. He knew David must have heard the news about the award already, and he hadn't even congratulated him.

At home, Iain went straight to bed. When he woke up four hours later, he felt much more refreshed. By the time he had showered, it was almost time for him to pick up Kirsty. On the way to Leith, Iain stopped at a small supermarket and picked up a bunch of flowers, regretting that he didn't think of ordering flowers from a florist beforehand.

The roads weren't busy, and Iain reached Joe's with fifteen minutes to spare.

When he walked into Joe's, Kirsty wasn't at her usual place behind the counter. All the staff turned and stared at him. Iain could almost feel the hostility. He walked towards the counter where Morag stood, watching him with a frown.

Iain felt almost hesitant to ask her, but if he wanted to see Kirsty, he didn't have much choice.

"Kirsty in the office?"

"No, she's not here," Morag muttered.

Iain frowned, "Wasn't she supposed to be working?"

"Yes, she was, but she left early."

Iain felt his heart clench. "Is she okay? Is she sick?"

"She's not sick," Morag answered, again abrupt.

Iain turned towards the door and said, "I'll go to her house."

"She's not there."

Iain sighed and turned back to Morag, "Where is she then?"

"I don't think it is any of your business."

Iain frowned, walking closer to the counter, "Morag, I may be wrong, but it feels as if you're angry with me. Please, tell me where Kirsty is and what the hell is going on?"

Morag folded her arms over her chest and glared at Iain. "You still ask? You two-timing..."

Iain stopped her, "What are you talking about?"

Morag grabbed a newspaper from the counter and threw it in front of Iain. He picked it up when the headline caught his eye, *'Edinburgh millionaire received a top award.'*

Iain turned the paper and cursed. It was a photo taken last night at the Business Circle Dinner. It was a clear photo of Iain, but he wasn't alone. Lydia Brickley, his ex, had insinuated herself in the picture. The tagline under the image read:

Local millionaire businessman Iain Young received the Young Businessman of the Year Award at the Annual Awards Ceremony of the Business Circle held in London last night. At his side was a London-based barrister, Lydia Brickley.

In the article, it further stated:

Mister Young and Miss Brickley had been a couple for almost two years before Mister Young had returned to Edinburgh to take over Young Incorporated after his father's passing last year. Had the couple rekindled their relationship? It might be the case. A source confirmed that Mister Young had stated last night he was ready to settle down and would announce it soon.

Iain cursed again. He threw the paper on the counter and said, "Some of it might be the truth, but it isn't what it looks like."

"So, you deny that the woman in the photo is your ex or that she was with you last night?" Morag demanded.

Iain glared at her, "Not that it has anything to do with you, but yes, I deny it. Has Kirsty seen this?"

"Yes, she has," Morag confirmed, still glaring at Iain.

"Morag, please, I need to speak to Kirsty."

Morag shook her head. "I'm sorry. I can't help you. Kirsty gave instructions not to give any information about her whereabouts to you."

Iain sighed and closed his eyes. What was he supposed to do now? He opened his eyes again when Morag mumbled, "I need the key to her apartment."

Iain clenched his jaw. Was this it? Was he not going to get a chance to explain?

He threw the flowers on the counter and took out his keys. Taking off the key to Kirsty's apartment, Iain felt as if his world was tumbling down. He slid the key to Morag with shaking hands. He wanted to turn towards the door when Morag bent down. When she got up, she held a plastic bag towards Iain, "I believe this is yours."

Iain didn't have to look to know what was in the bag. He knew it could only be the t-shirt and extra shaving kit, and the book he was busy reading and had left at Kirsty's place.

He took the bag from Morag and looked up at her, whispering, "She didn't even give me a chance."

12

Iain didn't wait for a response and turned to leave. If Kirsty wanted to humiliate him, she had done an excellent job.

Iain held his pose until he was back in his car. He dropped his head on his hands, clutching the steering wheel and took shuddering breaths. Iain sat there for an hour or even longer before he felt in control enough to start the car. He drove home, letting himself into the silent house.

He only managed it to the couch in the den where he sat, staring into space.

He hadn't declared his love yet. That was Iain's only consolation. What if he had and Kirsty rejected him like this? He wondered if he would have been able to stand more humiliation than he had already.

For the first time in months, Iain was alone. He wasn't ready to face anyone yet. After his pity party for one on Saturday, involving a bottle of single-malt whisky, Iain woke from the couch where he had fallen asleep during the night.

He sat for a while and then stood up. The pity party was over, and he needed to get on with his life. The only problem was that it would be a life without Kirsty.

He ignored the sudden flash of regret and walked up to his room. After a shower and a cup of tea, vowing to avoid coffee at all costs, Iain went to his study and worked. He ignored the messages and phone calls and focused on business.

He had to deal with Joe's. Kirsty Brown would not win this battle. He couldn't move Young's to Cairistìne Court when he knew Kirsty would be downstairs. Iain wouldn't be able to resist her. He knew that. His only option was to get rid of Joe's.

Iain swallowed another pang of regret and composed an e-mail. He didn't even read it through again before he mailed it off. The ball was now in Kirsty's court.

Iain put Joe's, Kirsty Brown and most other matters on the back burner when he received a phone call in the early hours of Monday morning. Four hours later, Iain stopped his car at the distillery near Keith that belonged to Young's. Since he had left Edinburgh, Iain had received regular updates about the fire that had necessitated this trip. He had expected to see a blast, but Iain had hoped that it was better news by the time he arrived. Even though half of Speyside's fire brigade was battling to contain the fire, it was still raging strong.

Iain lost unnecessary time in trying to convince the constable posted at the gate to let him in. When he was inside at last, after the constable had spoken to the plant manager, Iain could understand why they were reluctant to let anyone in. The area surrounding the inferno was a danger zone, and the fewer people in the vicinity, the better.

Not only did they have to battle dousing the fire, but they also had to prevent the fire from spreading to the other warehouses. Iain was philosophical when the fire chief had spoken to him later that day to commiserate with him. It could have been far worse. The explosion and subsequent fire happened in the early hours of the morning. There was no one in the warehouse and just the fact that nobody lost their lives in the inferno, was miraculous. Throughout the day, some firemen received treatment for exhaustion and smoke inhalation, but that was the only injuries.

The drizzle that started late on Monday night had been a godsend in helping the already exhausted firefighters to bring the fire under control, almost twenty-four hours after Iain got the first call.

During the day, Iain found out what had happened. According to the night manager, he and the guard were busy making coffee when they had heard an explosion. They went outside to investigate and found that the blast almost destroyed the one end and part of one side of the Number Four warehouse. They said it had all collapsed in about five minutes.

The fire could have been much worse. There were ten ware-houses at the plant with each one containing fifteen thou-sand barrels filled with about forty gallons of whisky. Because of the swift reaction of the night manager, the fire brigade had been quick to respond. On Tuesday afternoon, the Fire Chief started the investigation into the cause of the fire, but even now, four days later, there was no firm conclusion.

The fire had opened another assortment of problems at the distillery. It took Iain two more days to work through the grievances of the disgruntled staff, aimed at the English plant manager appointed a few months before his father's passing. Most of the complaints were legitimate, and Iain had to step in and fire him.

Iain had listened to the workers and appointed one of the older, more senior men as the new plant manager. Iain had to go to Skye to the other distillery owned by Young's. It took all Iain's effort to convince the manager at the Skye distillery to go to Speyside to train the appointed plant manager and help him settle in the new job.

THEY CALL it Blue Monday for a reason, Kirsty realised early on Monday morning. She could use all the clichés in the book to describe her morning so far, like getting out of the wrong side of the bed, which she literally did, because she had cried herself to sleep on the pillow that still carried a faint smell of Iain. She felt disoriented, and that feeling had stayed with her while she showered, using shower gel instead of shampoo and cutting herself while shaving her legs.

Maybe she shouldn't have opened her browser to read her e-mails before she had had her first cup of coffee. Iain's e-mail had spoiled that first cup which she usually savoured. She wondered why she had even hoped for an apology or an explanation. That e-mail was anything but that. Kirsty didn't have to read much of it before her temper got the better of her. She finished her cup of coffee before she replied, willing herself not to let her hurt and anger interfere with her business. It was now only business between her and Iain.

After she sent her answer, in which she had copied her lawyer, Kirsty had to congratulate herself on her response. She re-read it and felt satisfied that she hadn't allowed Iain Young to scare her.

Thank you for your E-mail.

I've indicated on previous occasions I'm not prepared to move Joe's. I've forwarded your correspondence to my lawyer, Mr Douglas Munroe. Should you wish to discuss the matter any further, please contact him.

Regards, Kirstine Brown

BY THE TIME she had arrived at Joe's, her day had already been a disaster but to find construction crews blocking the road in front of the building, was just enough to mess her day up further.

A canvas covered the front wall of the building. Members of the building crew were busy carrying supplies into the building so they could move their vehicles as soon as possible, according to the foreman to whom Kirsty had spoken.

Joe's was busy, more so than usual. The regulars speculated about what was happening with the building, but even though they asked her, Kirsty couldn't help. Iain had never spoken to her about his plans for the building, and she never asked.

Around eleven, Kirsty's heart sank. First Aileen arrived, then Graeme with an older woman at his side. They greeted Kirsty as friendly as usual and took a table in the corner.

They glanced at their watches, and Kirsty had a feeling they were waiting for Iain. She wasn't in the mood to confront Iain in Joe's and definitely not feeling as she did. Iain, however, appeared to be missing and after one more glance at her watch, Aileen stood up and walked towards Kirsty.

Kirsty could feel her spine stiffening while she watched the other woman's approach. Aileen was friendly enough, but her next words confirmed to Kirsty that Aileen didn't know that Iain had moved on. Aileen glanced at her watch, then the door before she asked Kirsty, "Do you know where Iain is? He was supposed to meet us here, but he's not at the house or the office."

"No," Kirsty answered stiffly.

Taking out her phone and glancing at the screen, Aileen tried again, "He's not answering his phone. Did he say anything over the weekend?"

Kirsty glared again at Aileen, "I haven't seen him."

Maybe something in Kirsty's voice registered with Aileen because she looked at her strangely. "You haven't seen him over the weekend? I thought he was with you?"

"No, maybe you should ask his girlfriend," Kirsty managed through clenched teeth.

Aileen frowned, "Girlfriend? What girlfriend? I thought you..."

Kirsty grabbed Saturday's paper, still lying under the counter where Kirsty had shoved it earlier this morning and put it in front of Aileen without a word. Aileen stared at the paper in shock. Iain had kept his happy news even from his siblings.

Aileen picked up the paper and read. When she finished, she looked up and asked, "May I take it?"

Kirsty nodded, "Please do. I don't need a reminder."

Aileen turned away when the older woman rushed up to her, "I've just spoken to Iain. He..."

Kirsty couldn't hear the rest of her words, because they were walking to the door where they joined Graeme, who had already settled their bill. All three of them looked concerned when they met at the door. They were still deep in conversation, just outside of Joe's. Kirsty could see when Aileen showed them the paper.

Both the older woman and Graeme shook their heads after they had looked at the paper. Graeme looked back at Joe's with a frown, before he handed the paper back to Aileen. Aileen and the other woman disappeared, and Graeme walked to the entrance of the building. When he came out a while later, Graeme was in the manager of the construction crew's company. They spoke for a few minutes before the construction manager disappeared into the building once more.

For the second time that day, Kirsty's heart sank when she saw Graeme walk away, then stopped and entered Joe's again. His eyes searched for Kirsty, and when he found her behind the counter, he walked towards her. He stopped in front of her and said, "Kirsty, that article..."

"I'm not interested, Graeme."

"But that..." Graeme tried again.

"I said I'm not interested. If you want to tell me that Iain isn't with Lydia, then you can save your breath. I saw his phone on Friday morning by accident. She phoned him early on Friday morning, and when he didn't answer, she sent a message where she confirmed seeing him in London on Friday night. I don't want to hear anything else from him."

Graeme shook his head, still not convinced, but Kirsty didn't give him a chance to say anything else because she carried on, "You can also tell your brother it doesn't matter what veiled threats he makes or offering me a million pounds, I'm not moving. Joe's is staying where it is. He isn't to contact me about it again, not in person or by e-mail. You have my lawyer's details."

Graeme frowned, "Has Iain told you what he planned for the building?"

"No. Why should he? I'm just the woman he slept with while he made plans on marrying someone else. Why should he discuss his business with me?"

"Kirsty, I don't understand what's going on. I've spoken to Iain on Friday night, and I know what he had planned for the building and Joe's. He..."

Kirsty interrupted him. "Well, that's great for you, but I'm not interested in anything your brother does anymore. He never mentioned any of his plans in all these months. Well, that was until yesterday's e-mail telling me he'll make sure that Joe's moved. I guess it would be embarrassing if your future wife finds out you slept with your tenant."

"Yesterday's e-mail?" Graeme asked, confused.

Kirsty took out her phone, opening her e-mail browser and the specific e-mail before she shoved it at Graeme. She heard his curse but ignored it.

He looked up with a grimace and asked, "May I forward it to myself?"

Kirsty nodded, "By all means. As I've said, you can speak to Dougie Munroe. I've already sent it to him so he might wait for your call."

With that, Kirsty turned and walked to her office, leaving a confused Graeme staring after her.

WHEN KIRSTY ARRIVED at Joe's on Tuesday morning, she was tired after she cried herself to sleep for the third night in a row. She felt irritated. All she did was cry. She knew it would happen. Didn't she prepare all these months for the time when Iain would break up with her? It might feel worse because she hadn't expected it to be so soon. Why had he been so cruel about it? That she didn't understand.

Unfortunately, Kirsty didn't even have time to dwell on her misery. When she switched on the coffee machine, she found that the device didn't build up any pressure. Kirsty sighed. It could only mean one thing, and that was that a valve broke. It would be cheaper to replace the valve than buying a new machine, but she couldn't understand how it had happened. She had noticed nothing wrong last night when they cleaned up. Maybe she didn't pay much attention because she felt so miserable.

In the meantime, she needed to make a plan. Sending a quick message to Morag, Kirsty rushed back to her apartment to get the one from home. It wasn't as big a machine like the one in the shop, but at least it would help. She had to take her car, so she dropped her machine off at the shop, where Morag was already waiting with her percolator. Today they might need to go the plunger route if it got too busy. With Morag's help, she loaded the coffee machine in her car and negotiated her way into the early morning traffic into Portobello.

She hoped her excellent record with her supplier would stand her in good stead today and that they could help her fix the machine. She knew Carlo had a stock of any replacements needed for the devices and his technicians would deal with the problem.

It was, however, almost lunchtime when Kirsty arrived back at Joe's with the fixed machine. She was worried but didn't let on to her staff. It was only after the lunchtime rush that Kirsty could speak to Morag and confided what Carlos' technician had told her—the damage to the machine wasn't because of the usual wear and tear. Someone had removed the valve.

Her bad luck didn't end there. On Wednesday morning, there was no water. When the building crew arrived at half-past eight, they found that someone had turned off the water at the mains. Kirsty couldn't access the mains, as the construction crew had cordoned it off for the renovations. By the time the water was back on, they had missed the morning rush, which contributed to a significant portion of their daily trade.

. . .

EVEN THOUGH STRUGGLING with the problems they faced at Joe's, Kirsty still had enough time to think. It bothered her that Iain hadn't mentioned the renovations or his plans for Cairistìne Court. Hell, it had bothered her the whole time they were dating, but she had always avoided talking business with Iain. It scared Kirsty that if she did, it would mean the end of their relationship. She tried to avoid the subject because the fool she was, she hoped to hold on to that happiness as long as possible.

Things were happening with the building as the old tenants moved out, but Iain had mentioned nothing. Kirsty suspected he too tried to avoid the subject.

Kirsty had to face the facts. Maybe Iain had hoped to make her soft so she will move, but she had a surprise for him. She would not give up yet.

When she arrived on Thursday morning and found no electricity, Kirsty burst into tears. Again, she phoned the foreman of the construction crew, who found that someone had forgotten to switch the power back on the previous night when they finished for the day. Even though it was cold enough, Kirsty had to throw away all the perishables. It was a health risk and something she couldn't take the chance of being contaminated. They had to clean the fridges and had to get the health inspector in before she could buy new supplies.

Kirsty told the health inspector that her grandfather had always believed that bad luck came in threes, and she hoped that it was the last one, explaining all the bad luck she had this week. That wasn't even mentioning Iain.

When the health inspector joked that it almost looked like someone didn't want her to do business, he planted a seed of suspicion in Kirsty's mind. When she thought about it, she realised that her problems started since Iain's crew worked on the building. Iain's e-mail on Sunday further stoked Kirsty's suspicions.

She had written an e-mail to the maintenance manager regarding her suspicions, but he only replied that she needed to prove her allegations. Kirsty knew she had no proof, but she promised herself to be more vigilant. She had talked to her staff, but it wasn't easy to keep an eye on everything. The crew came into the shop at odd times. She couldn't stop them from being there.

That evening, Kirsty promised herself that it would be the last time she cried over Iain. She had made a promise to her grandfather, and she planned to keep it for as long as she could. Iain might try to sabotage her to get her to move Joe's, but she would not lose this battle without a fight.

13

By the time Iain arrived back in Edinburgh on Friday morning, he was exhausted, to put it mildly. He hadn't had a good nights' sleep the last few days, not only because of the fire and stress but because he missed Kirsty. The initial anger Iain had felt on Saturday and Sunday had somehow dissipated throughout the week. Driving back to Edinburgh early on Friday morning, Iain knew he had to try one more time to speak to her.

He was so tired he could almost not lift his head. He had just come into the office an hour ago to report to Graeme and Aileen. When he finished here, he would speak to Kirsty.

He was in the middle of his report when there was a commotion at the door. The next moment Kirsty stormed in. She had black smudges over her face and clothes. Tears were streaming down her face. Iain was alert and jumped up asking concerned.

"What's wrong, Sweetheart?"

Kirsty had reached him by then, but instead of throwing herself into his arms as Iain had hoped, she pushed him so hard against the chest that Iain's tired body staggered against the conference table. She followed him, stabbing him against the chest. "How could you, Iain Young? I never thought you would do this."

Iain sighed, "What are you talking about, Kirsty?"

He could see that even though she was crying, she was furious. She shouted, "You sabotaged me. You thought if I can't run my business, I won't be able to pay my rent and I have to give up, didn't you?"

"Sweetheart, I don't know what you're talking about," Iain tried again.

"I'm not your sweetheart, so stop calling me that. You know what I'm talking about, but I've news for you. I won't let you off the hook. The valve missing from the coffee machine, the lack of water, and the power loss I may not prove, but the fire chief found that the fire this morning was intentional. You'll hear from my lawyer."

With those words, Kirsty stormed out of the door. Iain couldn't even follow her as he was so tired. He turned his head to his brother and sister in confusion. "Do you know what she's talking about?"

Both shook their heads, as confused as Iain. Iain barked at Moira, "Get Mackay in here."

A few minutes later, a satisfied Walter Mackay walked into the office. He snickered at Iain, "I've noticed our Miss Brown just leaving. Did it work? Is she giving up?"

Iain felt as if he would explode. He took a shuddering breath, willing himself to calm down. He glanced at Graeme and Moira. Iain noticed that Moira moved to the digital recorder and pressed the record button. Graeme moved to stand next to Iain and so did Aileen.

Mackay didn't know Iain, because Iain's voice was deceptively calm when he asked, "Could you explain what is going on, Mr Mackay. Did what work?"

"The sabotaging," Mackay admitted. Iain thought the man must be stupid to confess to such a crime without even thinking about the consequences.

"I got Jack, one of the maintenance crew, to remove the valve of the coffee machine and to turn the water off. He also 'forgot' to put the electricity back on the night before and this morning, he played with the wires of a toaster, you know, to cause a spark so they couldn't use the machine."

Iain felt the blood roar in his ears. Before he could stop himself, he grabbed Mackay by the front of his shirt and shouted, "Are you out of your fucking mind? You could have had people killed!"

Mackay frowned, "I thought that's what you wanted. I've seen the e-mail you've sent her in which you told her you'd make sure Joe's won't be able to stay in that building."

Iain frowned, and then remembered the e-mail he sent to Kirsty on Sunday. He scowled at Mackay, "How did you see it? I never copied that e-mail to you, and neither was it on the server."

Mackay flushed when he glanced at Graeme.

Graeme explained, "I may have put it on the server. I spoke to Kirsty on Monday, and after she showed me the e-mail, I forwarded it to myself, although I'm not sure how you could see it, Mackay. You're not supposed to have access to management's e-mails."

Iain felt as if he could explode. It might be better that he didn't know how Mackay got hold of that e-mail. He was so furious he could do the man harm, so he threw Mackay away from him and took a few deep breaths, thinking hard.

Iain turned to the other occupants of the room, "Aileen, phone the police. Graeme, fire Mackay with immediate effect. He will have to wait for any funds owed to him until we have determined the damage at Joe's. Deduct the costs Kirsty and Joe's have suffered from any pay-out he might have received. Moira, get security up here to take care of Mackay until the police can take him away."

By this time, Mackay's swagger and smile had disappeared. Iain guessed he didn't know how angry he was, because he said to Iain, "You should have thanked me. She may be a good lay, but she would have cost us money, not being able to sell the building."

This time Iain didn't stop. Before Mackay knew what was going on, Iain's fist hit him straight in the mouth. When Mackay staggered backwards, Iain grunted, "You're a moron, Mackay but you do not talk about my future wife like that. It shows how little you care about what's going on. For your information, even if I had sold the building, you or the company would not have benefited from it. Cairistìne Court is my private property. The company only manages it for me and—not that it would concern you anymore—I'm moving our headquarters there."

The security guards came in, and Graeme gave them instructions on what to do. When they left, Iain paced, thinking on his feet.

"Aileen, phone the foreman in charge of the construction crew and the fire chief, asking them to meet me in an hour in front of Joe's. Moira, ask David to meet me out in front in ten minutes with the biggest bunch of red roses he can find. Then phone the jeweller and tell him I'll be around in fifteen minutes to pick up the ring, whether or not it's clean."

Moira left, but his siblings didn't. When Iain wanted to leave to go to his office, Graeme stopped him.

"What's going on, Iain?"

Iain frowned, "With what?"

"With you, Kirsty, and Lydia," Aileen demanded.

Iain cursed. "You've seen the article. It's not what it looks like, and Kirsty didn't give me a chance to explain. I don't understand how she could so readily believe it."

"I know the article insinuated something else," Graeme said, "I've been there, remember. Anyway, I think I know why Kirsty thought it was the truth. She saw your phone with a message from Lydia on Friday morning. According to her, the phone had rung, and as it was early, she thought it might be urgent and went to answer it. She was too late. She noticed several missed calls from Lydia too. Just when she wanted to put the phone down, a message came in from Lydia. Kirsty could only read the first part of the message, she admitted but combined with the newspaper article, I guess it was enough evidence for her."

Iain took out his phone and went back to the messages from Lydia. As Iain answered none of them and hadn't even read them, he didn't know which one Graeme referred to. Scrolling through them, he found the only one that could be the one Kirsty might have seen. It read: *See you tonight. I miss you and hope to talk to you. With my Dad's help, I've got an invite to the Dinner.*

Iain stared at it before he handed his phone to Graeme. "This message, I guess. I haven't even answered Lydia. I worried something like that would happen, and that's why I hoped Kirsty could go with me. Since that first article in the paper about my nomination, Lydia kept on calling me. I made a mistake the first time to take her call, but she didn't want to take no for an answer, even after I told her I'm no longer interested."

"I heard you were saying that to her, but I don't think that's the only problem. That you never told Kirsty what you planned with Cairistìne Court and Joe's, also contributed to Kirsty's hurt and mistrust. You must do a lot of grovelling, Bro'."

"I know that, Graeme. Do you have the document I want to give Kirsty?"

Graeme nodded, so Iain told him and Aileen, "Okay, I need a quick shower. I can't propose in this state. Meet me at the car. I may need you as a backup."

KIRSTY LOOKED up when the door opened, expecting the fire chief to return. She didn't expect the enormous bouquet of red roses entering first, and then a whole entourage of men and one woman following in the bouquet bearer's wake. She didn't have to wonder who the bouquet bearer was, because right behind him was his brother and sister.

Kirsty stared. When Iain lowered the bouquet, Kirsty attacked "If you think a bunch of flowers will soften me up, Iain Young, you're making a big mistake. I've already notified my lawyer."

Iain sighed, "That's not what it is for, but I realised I have some explaining to do. The flowers are just part of my apology. Please give me a chance."

"You must be joking," Kirsty muttered and turned away, although she didn't get very far when Iain's voice stopped her. Instead of speaking to Kirsty, Iain cleared his throat and raised his voice.

The voices around them quieted down when he said, "Some of you may know who I am, but others don't so let me introduce myself. I'm Iain Young, owner of Cairistìne Court. You may believe that I'm responsible for the sabotage that occurred in Joe's this week, but I need to clarify I did not know of it, and neither had my brother and sister. One individual in my company took it upon himself, hoping that he would benefit from the sale. I got confirmation of the arrest of both him and the person responsible for the sabotage. His act was born out of greediness and stupidity. He would never benefit because this building belongs to me and not to Young's. I'm not selling the building. Young's are moving to Cairistìne Court as soon as they complete the renovations."

Kirsty turned around to face Iain when his words reached her brain. He was moving his company to Cairistìne Court. How long ago did he plan that? Not that it mattered. He still wanted Joe's to move.

Kirsty's voice was quiet when she confirmed, "You are moving your company upstairs?"

Iain nodded. Kirsty folded her arms around her chest and demanded from Iain, "Since when?"

Iain turned his head towards her, a flush creeping up his face. "We decided in July."

Kirsty closed her eyes, but then her anger got the better of her, "You decided to move your company here even before we dated?"

Iain nodded, and Kirsty demanded, "Why, Iain? Why did you decide to move Young's here, to this building?"

Iain swallowed, but then he admitted, "I want to move my company here to Leith so I could be closer to my future wife. I planned to give half of Cairistìne Court to her as a wedding present."

Kirsty almost burst into tears, but she wouldn't give Iain the satisfaction. She didn't give him a chance to elaborate. He didn't have to, because Kirsty knew whom he planned to marry. She'd seen the paper. She only needed to understand why he never told her that. Not that it mattered anymore. She definitely could not bear it, seeing him every day when he was married.

Maybe it was best she close Joe's. It wasn't only the loss of income this week and the renovations she had to do after the fire. She had her inheritance, and the insurance should pay. The question was: Was it worth it?

Kirsty couldn't speak. She stared at Iain without answering. She then moved her gaze away from him and let it slide over Joe's. The regular customers were watching her, but Kirsty didn't have the energy to talk to them. She ignored Iain and turned to Morag, who was watching her with a similar anxious expression as the customers and the rest of the staff. The next moment Peter walked in. Morag must've let him know what was going on.

Peter ignored Iain and went to stand next to Kirsty, sliding his arm around her shoulders. Kirsty felt so defeated, she only let her head drop to his shoulder, in time to hear him whispering, "I'm taking you to my Mum. She's at the cottage. Don't worry about Joe's. Morag and I will take care of everything for now. Take a few days. It will help if you go away. If there is any paperwork for the insurance you need to sign, I'll bring it to you. I've taken the day off to take care of you, just like you and Joe did for us when my father died."

Kirsty nodded against his chest. She knew he and Morag could deal with Joe's. She would only be a phone call away. She needed time to work through everything that had happened in the last few months, and she needed to do it away from Joe's and Iain.

When Peter turned her away, he took her bag from Morag and whispered to his fiancé, "I'll be back as soon as I can."

Like a fool, Kirsty took one more glance at Iain. She shouldn't have, because at that moment she almost felt sorry for him. She didn't know why. He was the reason she was giving up the one thing she and her grandfather had worked hard for so long.

She didn't want to fight. Not today. She needed the weekend to lick her wounds at least, and then she'd be back to close Joe's up.

She only whispered, with tears sliding down her cheeks, making an even bigger mess of her already soot-covered face, "You've won, Iain. I give up."

"Kirsty..."

She heard his pleading voice, but she had to leave. She walked out of Joe's, grateful for Peter's supporting arm around her shoulders.

14

I ain stared in shock at Kirsty's back, the arm of the man he had seen with her in the pub months ago, around her shoulders.

He dropped the flowers on the floor, uncaring of what happened to it. He felt Graeme's hand on his shoulder, and he looked at his brother. The events of the last week became too much. Iain swayed.

Maybe it was the shock. Perhaps he was just so damn tired, but Iain felt as if all the energy had drained out of him.

He didn't have to say anything. Iain and Aileen left Joe's, but Iain hardly knew it. He didn't know how he got to the car, or how they got to his house. Iain only woke up on Saturday afternoon.

When he drifted downstairs after a reviving shower, the heaviness hadn't left yet.

He wasn't surprised to find his siblings in the kitchen when Iain went to search for something to drink. Aileen got up and poured him a mug of coffee. When Iain lifted the cup to his mouth, he smelled the familiar aroma, and he closed his eyes. His hand shook, and he put the mug down on the table, staring at it. He looked up at his siblings and asked, "What the hell happened?"

Iain got irritated with his brother. He saw the smile lurking at Graeme's mouth when he answered, "A whole lot of shit, Bro', but it's not over. Let me fill you in, and then we can regroup. This time you need our help."

Iain sighed. "I wish I knew how. You heard her. She lost the thing that was the most important to her, and she blames me for it. I don't think she'll ever forgive me. Hell, she didn't even want to listen when I tried to explain that I wanted to give her half of Cairistine Court after we got married."

He shook his head in resignation, "No, I don't know if I can go through this again. It was the second time she pushed me away since that photo appeared."

Graeme laughed, but before he could say anything, his phone rang. "Hiya," he answered.

He listened to the person speaking on the other side, nodding and smiling. "That's awesome. Thanks. Listen, we need to talk and figure things out. You busy?"

Graeme listened while the other person spoke again before he said, "Okay, we're at Iain's house in Cramond. Would you like to come here? Be prepared to stay over, as we have a lot to figure out."

Again, he listened, and then he said, "All right. I'll send you the directions. See you."

Iain scowled at him, "Who did you invite over so freely?"

Graeme shook his head, "You'll see. Let's try to figure this out before they get here."

Iain turned to Aileen, "Do you know what's going on?"

She nodded with a smile, "*Aye,* but it's Graeme's show."

With a sigh, Iain turned back to Graeme, "Then get on with it."

"Okay, let's start with the most important part. Do you love Kirsty?"

"I do. Why else would I want to marry Kirsty?"

"Then why have you never told her how you feel?"

Iain sighed. "Stupidity? Fear? I don't know. I thought it was too soon, I guess. Geez, guys. You know me. How many times had I made the mistake of falling in love too soon, telling the women only to find out it wasn't love at all. Hell, look what happened with Lydia. I thought I was in love with her, and I told her so. Two years down the line I can't stand her."

Graeme nodded, "I guess that's understandable to be wary then. So, what's different with Kirsty? Why are you so sure she's the one you want to marry? Who says you won't feel it is a mistake in a few months?"

Iain stared at the now cold coffee in the mug. "I don't know. It just is. Kirsty is..."

He took a deep breath before he looked up at his brother, "I don't know how to put it but Kirsty... With her, I can be myself. She doesn't expect me to be 'on' the whole time. She doesn't mind just snuggling up next to me reading a book or watching a movie. She doesn't mind not going to fancy restaurants or expensive holidays or wearing the latest designer gear. I know I can afford those things, but that's not important. You know me. I prefer reading a book instead of socialising. With Kirsty... I learned so much about being with a person. I love going for a walk on the beach and eating fish and chips out of a newspaper wrapping instead of going to a five-star restaurant. She is just... Kirsty is the one I could talk to about almost anything. She doesn't 'expect' or 'want' anything from me, except me. She completes my soul. "

Aileen and Graeme glanced at each other before Aileen said, "I hope one day to find a man who loves me as much as you love Kirsty. That was beautiful, Iain," she added, wiping the tears from her cheeks.

She took a deep breath and then added, "I think we know how to get Kirsty back."

"How?" Iain frowned. "I failed her. I did not protect the one thing that is the most important to her. She lost Joe's, and I don't think she'll ever forgive me."

Aileen pointed out, "By giving her back the one thing that is the most important to her, except you, I guess."

"I doubt your last statement, Alee," Iain sighed, using Aileen's childhood pet name. "Just as I never told her how I felt, she had never told me, and after what happened, I doubt she ever will."

"She will. Of that I'm certain," Aileen reassured him.

Iain got up to pour out the now cold coffee and made a fresh pot. When the aroma of the brewed coffee filled the kitchen, Iain closed his eyes. The memories associated with it made his heart clench. He leaned his arms on the counter and let his head drop to his arm.

It hurt. Nothing in Iain's life ever had hurt so much—not even losing his parents or giving up the career he worked so hard for.

Images of moments he shared with Kirsty flashed before his eyes.

Iain was so lost in his memories that he didn't even hear the doorbell ring or realise that Graeme had left the kitchen. Only when Graeme touched his arm and said, "Iain, we have visitors," that he opened his eyes and turned towards Graeme's voice.

Iain was unaware that the misery reflected in his eyes, so he didn't know to hide it. When he recognised the two visitors, Iain stiffened. They were the last two people he had expected.

His eyes moved between Morag and the dark-haired man with whom Kirsty had left yesterday. Iain said nothing. He didn't know what to say. The man stepped forward, holding out his hand to Iain, "I'm Peter Moriarty, Morag's fiancé."

When Iain frowned, Peter added, "And Kirsty's best friend since we were five years old."

Iain exhaled, and then he stretched out to shake Peter's hand, "I guess you know who I am."

Peter nodded, a slight smile playing on his lips. "Yes, I do, and I believe you and Kirsty need our help."

Iain snorted. The man wasn't beating around the bush, but he wasn't sure what they could do to fix what went wrong between him and Kirsty.

He turned, taking out mugs from the cupboard and putting them on the table where Graeme had left the milk and sugar. When the percolator finished making its gurgling sounds, Iain picked up the jug and refilled his cup before he put the coffee on the table and told his guests, "Help yourself," indicating to the pitcher.

He turned back to the counter, switched off the machine and took his place at the table.

When they all sat back with their mugs, Morag and Peter looked at each other and chuckled, "This is fitting. Joe had always said good ideas start with great coffee."

Iain didn't feel much like laughing. He wasn't sure what was going on, and he was anyway too anxious. He looked up at Peter and Morag, his eyes resting on Morag a little bit longer.

"How is Kirsty?"

Morag smiled, "As miserable as you."

Iain sighed, and then he added, "I don't know how to fix things."

Graeme cleared his throat, "I think we do," he said, glancing at Aileen, Morag and Peter before he looked back at Iain. "As Aileen said earlier before you got lost in your memories and your misery again, the one way to get Kirsty back is to give her the one thing, apart from you, that is important to her, and that's Joe's."

Iain flinched. He never even asked about the damage caused by the fire. He now had to know.

"How bad is the damage in Joe's?"

Aileen opened the folder and took out a few photos. "Not as bad as we first feared."

Iain studied the photos. Aileen was right. After the fire at the distillery, this wasn't as bad as he feared, but it would still set Kirsty back.

"Does she have insurance?"

Morag nodded. "Yes, she has, and the surveyors had already been in yesterday afternoon to assess the damage."

"Then why did she say she couldn't go on?" Iain frowned.

The four of them glanced between themselves before Morag said, "Well, it wasn't just the fire. The fire was just the last straw, I guess. Added to the unexpected expenses in getting the coffee machine fixed and replacing all the stock we lost when the power was off, we also had a loss of income for the last five days. I don't know when we can fix the kitchen, and it might take weeks. Kirsty might have the funds but not the will to go on. Or rather, she has funds, but they are all tied up in investments which will take time to get released. She will have to use all her disposable income to pay the rent and the staff, but she won't have an income. Not until we fix the kitchen and the health inspector gives us the go-ahead."

Iain cursed. He wished he could get hold of Mackay. "I'll forfeit the rent. I would do it anyway when..."

He stopped and shook his head. It would not happen now, but he would have cancelled Kirsty's rent when they were married. How could she pay rent to herself?

Anyway, Young's would carry the upkeep of the building. Iain didn't even take money from his company. It wasn't as if he needed it.

Morag interrupted his thoughts again, "You know that this isn't the reason Kirsty has given up, don't you?"

Iain frowned, "Why else would she feel it necessary to give up Joe's?" he asked, confused.

"You," Morag admitted. "Kirsty doesn't want to be in the same building as you."

Iain flinched. Morag's confirming Iain's thoughts, hurt. Would he be able to work there, knowing she was only two floors down?

Would he be able to go into Joe's? Iain shook his head. He wouldn't, and he couldn't. Not knowing she was there and she hated him. Without even consulting his siblings, he decided, "Then Young's can stay where we are. I don't want her to give up Joe's."

"Iain?"

Iain looked at Morag when she said his name. He could see the small smile lurking at her mouth when she asked, "Why would you do that? You've gone to a lot of expense to renovate the building."

"It doesn't matter. I don't want Kirsty to feel uncomfortable. She must keep Joe's."

"Why?"

Iain clenched his jaw. "Because Joe's is important to her. I want her to be happy, and Joe's make her happy."

"I'm asking again, Iain. Why? Why would you do that for her?"

Iain took a deep breath, "Because I love her, and I wouldn't be able to work there knowing she is downstairs, and she hates me."

He closed his eyes, fighting the sudden onslaught of desolation that wanted to overwhelm him. Just saying it was making it more real.

He didn't hear Morag's voice. It was only her hand on his arm that made him realise she was talking again. Iain opened his eyes, looking at her when she repeated, "She doesn't hate you, Iain."

Iain didn't know what to say, the thoughts rushing through him. If she doesn't hate him...

No, he couldn't think that. He couldn't hope and dream again but what if... He had to know, "Then why would Kirsty give up Joe's if I was working upstairs?"

Morag and Peter glanced at each other, and this time Peter answered, "Because she loves you too much to see you with your wife. She would rather leave."

Iain jumped up, yelling frustrated "What wife? She's the one I want to marry. No one else!"

Peter's words registered, and he stopped his tirade. He turned back to Peter and demanded, "Wait. What did you say?"

Peter grinned, "I wondered when you would register what I've said."

"She told you that?" Iain asked, much calmer than only minutes ago. "When?"

Peter nodded, "Yes, she told me. Two weeks ago and again last night."

Iain sank back in the chair. He put both hands over his face and dragged them down while he exhaled. When he opened his eyes, he glanced between the four people who were watching him with amusement before he said, "I need to see her."

Peter nodded but dashed Iain's hopes, "Not yet. She's still too upset. I've taken her to my mother near Hawick."

"Until when?" Iain demanded with a frown.

"Until we can convince her not to give up Joe's. I've convinced her to give it a week. I told her I'll come and pick her up next Saturday."

Iain leaned his elbows on the table, stapling his fingers in front of his face. He might have a chance, but then he would need all the help he could get.

He nodded, "Okay, a week. I'll grant Kirsty that, but after that, I'll get her myself. In the meantime, we have work to do."

He studied the photos Aileen had given him earlier and knew what he had to do.

"Aileen, pull the renovators from the building. I need them to start at Joe's on Monday. I'll pay them double, but I want the job done before Kirsty comes back. We will give Joe's a facelift. I don't want to change it, but it needs a lick of paint. The electricians and plumbers can also make sure that everything is up to standard. Our biggest problem is the kitchen. Will we be able to get someone to redo the kitchen at such short notice?"

He studied the photos again. "I think the kitchen anyway needed a do-over. It looks old-fashioned."

Peter chuckled, taking a folder Morag had pulled from her oversized handbag. "I think I can help there."

He opened the folder and slid a piece of paper over to Iain. "It will cost you, but I can guarantee you we will finish it by Friday."

When Iain studied the document, Peter said, "I'm working for the same design company as Olivia out in Portobello. Joe got us in last year to re-design the kitchen, and we gave him a quote. He wanted to do it this year, but, he passed away before he could do that. Kirsty and I had worked on it. Apart from the food kitchen, we also would have modernised the coffee bar, but would have kept the ambience of the shop."

Iain nodded. "You say Kirsty approved the designs?"

Peter nodded, "Yes, her signature is on it."

"How soon can you start?"

"Monday, but are you sure? Did you look at the price? It's steep, especially for such short notice. My staff would have to work overtime to complete it on time."

"I don't care how much it costs. Just do it," Iain instructed.

"Okay, I'll pull my crew in to start on Monday morning.

Iain tapped his fingers on the table, thinking hard. "What about your staff, Morag? We also need to get all the valuables out of Joe's before the crew can get in on Monday."

"I'm prepared to go in, and I'm certain the staff would go in too. We can pack away the books and photographs and all the other decorations."

"I'll come and help," Iain volunteered. Peter and his siblings echoed his offer.

"We need to take photographs of where everything in Joe's is. I want to put the photographs back in the same place they were. The same needs to happen with books and everything else. We must get boxes."

"No need," said Graeme. "I already got some at the office preparing for our move. We can use that.

Morag took out a notebook and pen and made notes.

"I am worried about something, Morag," Iain said, getting her attention.

"What is it?"

"I'm worried about Ellie and the others. I don't want them to suffer too. Your staff would also lose out.

"Why don't you hire a mobile coffee kitchen or something? It's only for the week," Peter suggested. "That way, the chef can still prepare sandwiches, etcetera, and the staff can take turns working there. It wouldn't be ideal, but it would be better than nothing."

Iain nodded. "Aileen, can you see if you can get something at short notice?"

For the rest of the afternoon and until late that evening, the five of them made plans.

15

Kirsty looked out of the window, watching the mist swirl over the hills. It had been like this the whole week since she arrived in Hawick. It had done little to lift her mood. She had been crying most of the time, much to her frustration. Kirsty wished she could stop thinking about everything, but it didn't matter how much she told herself to stop crying, she still did.

It wasn't only about losing Joe's. She still cried about Iain, now realising how significant a portion of her life he had occupied the last few months.

She had known that Iain would get married to someone else but had always hoped that she didn't have to witness it. She couldn't run Joe's, seeing Iain every day knowing he belonged to someone else.

She had warned herself not to get attached too much to Iain in her life, but the reality of losing him was so much worse.

Peter had warned her not to make hasty decisions about Joe's, but Kirsty had to think about it. Morag had promised to take the week to do an inventory and get quotations to get the kitchen replaced, but it would be all in vain.

She didn't know what she would do if she had to close Joe's. Kirsty wasn't even sure she wanted to stay in Edinburgh. No, maybe she must do what Morag and Olivia had done and travel, working where she can.

She sighed. She couldn't think about it all. She turned away from the window and finished packing the clothes she had brought with her.

Peter would be here later. He told his mother he was completing a project and might be late, but he had his key. They would leave tomorrow just after lunch, as he still wanted to visit with her.

Kirsty couldn't begrudge him that, but she would have liked to get back to Edinburgh. She needed to go to Joe's and say goodbye on her own.

She had already said goodnight to Peter's mother, and after she closed her suitcase, she crept into bed. She didn't even hear Peter come in, because by then she had yet again cried herself to sleep.

She knew she looked terrible the following morning. Trust Peter to be honest when he saw her. "No, girl. This won't do," he said after he hugged her. "I think you need a boost. When's the last time you've been to a hairdresser?"

Kirsty sighed, "Ages ago, and no, I can't think about it now. I need to let the staff go next week, and my savings are running low."

"Nonsense. It's my treat. I've promised you a big birthday present, and as your birthday is only a few days away, a special treat at the salon could be my present to you."

Kirsty knew she would not argue. She didn't feel like having a makeover, but maybe it would make her feel better. Without waiting for a reply, Peter walked off to make a call. A few minutes later, he came back and said, "It's arranged. We'll leave here just after lunch. Morag made an appointment for you. I'll drop you off at the salon."

"Can I go to Joe's first?" she asked.

Peter shook his head, "There won't be much time. I'll rather take you afterwards. We need to pick up Morag at Joe's anyway and then we can go out for a meal, or something."

Kirsty groaned. She didn't have the energy to go out. She would need to find an excuse before then. She would have to go back to Joe's tomorrow to say goodbye. Monday she would contact Dougie Munroe.

It was almost four pm when Kirsty walked out of the salon to Peter's waiting car, bursting for the bathroom. She had enough coffee while she was in the salon to keep her awake for the rest of the week.

It felt like everything took forever. Not only had Kirsty had her hair done, but Morag had also booked a manicure, pedicure and facial for her. If her heart didn't feel as if it was breaking, she would have enjoyed the experience more. At least she looked good on the outside, Kirsty thought. Inside, was another matter...

Peter parked just in front of Joe's. There were only a couple of lights on in the back, so Morag must be in the office. Kirsty got out with a heavy heart and looked at Joe's while Peter locked his car. When she felt his presence next to her, she walked to the entrance. Peter didn't wait for Kirsty to get out her key but rapped on the door a few times.

It was only a minute or two before Morag opened the door, enveloping Kirsty in a big hug, kissed Peter and hustled them both inside.

The light was dim inside Joe's, but Kirsty knew the place like the back of her hand. A few steps inside, Kirsty stopped. Something was different. At first, she stood still, trying to figure out what had triggered the feeling, but she realised she couldn't put her finger on it. She walked towards the light switch and flipped the button. Her eyes closed, shielding itself from the sudden brightness. She didn't even have to open them to tell that her instincts were right. Something was different inside Joe's.

She took a deep breath and opened her eyes.

If you didn't know Joe's as well as she did, you wouldn't have noticed the difference, but Kirsty did—not only the fact that the walls had a new lick of paint. Whoever did it, had re-sanded the floors- and it looked fresh. The photos and books were still there, although, when Kirsty inspected it, there were more photos on the walls than there had been before. She turned around, and she pulled in her breath.

The coffee bar now had the design she and Peter had worked on before Joe's passing. Kirsty walked around, touching the wooden countertops. It looked even better than she could ever have imagined.

Without knowing it, tears were streaming down her face.

She turned to Peter, shaking her head, "It was a waste of money. I can't keep Joe's. Not anymore. Why did you do it?"

Peter shook his head, "It wasn't me. It was him."

"Him?" Kirsty asked, frowning. She noticed Peter indicating his head to a space behind her, and she turned.

Iain.

Why did he do it?

"Why, Iain? I told you I couldn't stay here anymore. I have to break my promise to Joe, but I can't stay here if I know that you..."

Kirsty turned and rushed to the door, but Iain's voice stopped her from storming out. She turned her head to face him when he pleaded, "Kirsty wait. Please listen."

She saw how he took a deep breath before he added, his voice husky, "I've said I want to give Cairistìne Court to my future wife."

Kirsty flinched, but Iain didn't give her a chance to say anything. "I have a wee problem with that."

Someone asked from behind Kirsty, "What's the problem?"

Iain grimaced, although Kirsty could see he still looked tense. He licked his lips and said, "I haven't told the woman I hope to marry that I love her and want to marry her. I thought she needed time, but I realise now I was stupid. I should have done it a long time ago when I knew she was the one."

The same person who asked the previous question, sounding like Major Maguire, shouted, "Then why don't you tell her?"

Iain took the last step separating him and Kirsty, and he said so softly, only she could hear, while holding out a bunch of flowers to her, "I'll do it now."

Kirsty didn't take the flowers because she didn't see his action. She stared at Iain's face in shock and then turned away from him. She couldn't witness that.

Someone stepped in front of her, putting a hand out to stop her from opening the door. It wasn't Iain, because Kirsty knew his touch. She frowned confused. Where had everyone come from? She looked up at Graeme. Iain's brother held out a paper to Kirsty.

Kirsty stared at Graeme before her eyes flitted to the paper and again back to his face. His voice was gentle when he almost pleaded with her, "I know my brother can be daft sometimes, but his heart is in the right place. Please read that."

Kirsty blinked twice, then looked down at the document Graeme held out. She took it, her hands shaking and read.

She breathed in and re-read it, and again. The words started to make sense, and then Kirsty's eyes caught the date next to the three signatures.

Iain had signed his intent to transfer half of Cairistìne Court over to Kirsty with Graeme and Dougie Munroe as witnesses—two weeks before he took her to his house for the first time. Kirsty looked up to find Graeme still watching her. He nodded sagely.

Kirsty turned and found that Joe's was full. She fleetingly wondered where they all had come from, but it didn't matter. She needed to figure out what it meant, and she wanted to be alone to do that. As Graeme was still blocking her way to the exit, Kirsty made a beeline for the only other door, and that's to the kitchen.

She didn't leave, though.

Even in her dazed and confused state, Kirsty didn't miss the state of the kitchen.

When she had left the previous Friday, it was a mess caused by the fire.

It was anything but that now.

It was beautiful and what she had dreamed it would look like. Her eyes tried to take everything in, but when it fell on the large blackboard on the wall, Kirsty burst into tears.

In large, bold letters, the words could leave Kirsty in no doubt that what she had read in that document wasn't a figment of her imagination. She re-read the words and sighed. It was beautiful, and it was perfect.

Kirsty, I love you. Will you please marry me? Iain

She needed to find him and turned around to rush back into Joe's. She didn't have to. Iain was right there, kneeling on one knee and holding out a small jewellery box towards her.

"My brother is right. I've acted foolish, and I'm sorry. I love you, Kirstine Brown, with every fibre of my being. I know I should have said it sooner, but I love you and have done so for a long time. I guess... I guess I loved you even before I knew you and even before we dated. I want to spend the rest of my life with you, having children with you, growing old with you. I want to watch old movies with you, walk on the beach, sharing long talks and glasses of red wine. I want to explore, discover with you, but most of all, I want to love you. Will you please marry me?"

Kirsty swallowed her tears. "What about Lydia?"

Iain scowled, "There is a reason she's called an ex. I didn't go with her to dinner. She wangled an invitation through her father. I made it clear to her that night, in front of my brother and a few others, that I'm not interested in rekindling our relationship. I think my exact words were that I'd met the woman I want to marry and I'm planning to propose soon."

Kirsty took a deep breath. Iain still had a few things to explain, but that didn't matter now. The words on that paper and the blackboard behind her proved that Iain had planned this for a while.

She knew only one word was enough for now, and that was, "Yes."

As soon as she managed the one word through her tears, Iain slid the ring on her finger. Kirsty couldn't even admire it, for Iain stood up and pulled her into his arms.

Before he kissed her, she protested, "The others...," but Iain grinned and murmured back, "Forget about them. I missed you. I love you," and then his mouth claimed hers.

A long time later, Iain pulled away far enough for Kirsty to whisper, "I love you, Iain."

He smiled, claiming her mouth again in a sweet kiss. He lifted his head and whispered against her mouth, "You taste like coffee. You know you got me hooked with that first cup. I've since then acquired a taste for coffee—and you."

It was a long, long, long time later they rejoined the others in Joe's, where somehow, bottles of champagne had appeared.

"Were you that sure I would say yes?" Kirsty asked Iain with a smile.

"Oh, hell, no. I wasn't sure of anything," Iain exclaimed.

Kirsty brushed a kiss over his mouth and asked, "How did you do all this?" meaning Joe's.

"With the help of friends and family. Bribing contractors. You know, the usual thing," he laughed.

Iain took her hand and pulled her towards the one wall with photos.

"We even put your photos back in the exact position they had been. But here," Iain added, pulling Kirsty to the other wall, "we created a wall for new photos, for new memories. We've added a few for you, but over the years we can add more."

Kirsty stared at the photos. There were photos of her with Major Maguire and Ellie taken at the Veteran's Ball. Kirsty and the staff. Kirsty, Peter's mom and Peter and Kirsty with her grandfather.

Tucked between the others, was one of her and Iain, a selfie he had taken one day right here in Joe's.

Kirsty had no words. Her heart was too full for that. She turned to Iain, only managing a brief thank you before she pulled his head down towards her to kiss him.

Iain and Joe's. What more could a woman want?

Oh, yes, coffee.

Iain, Joe's and coffee...

Kirsty sighed against his mouth and pulled away only far enough to murmur, "I love you, Iain Young."

She swallowed his answer with her kiss, but it didn't matter. Kirsty didn't need him to say the words. His actions, giving her back Joe's, was proof of his love.

EPILOGUE
CHRISTMAS DAY

Kirsty stretched, and then cuddled under the blanket again. Iain's hand slipped around her middle. She could feel the unfamiliar ridge of his wedding band rubbing over her stomach. She turned to face him, looking into the bluest eyes which were gazing so tenderly back into hers.

Iain looked at her like that last night when they exchanged their vows in front of the judge, an old friend of his father.

There were few people at their wedding, but they both preferred it like that. The most important people in their lives were there. The relatively short list included his siblings, Chrissie and David, the groundsman and his wife, Duncan and Rab, Moira and her husband, Morag and Peter, Olivia and her son, Kirsty's chef and his partner, Ellie and Major Maguire and Dougie Munroe and his wife.

The ceremony was short but still romantic. It snowed just after dinner to tie in with the romantic atmosphere. Before

Dougie and his wife left, Dougie had handed an envelope over to Iain and Kirsty.

Kirsty had almost burst into tears because she had recognised her grandfather's sprawling handwriting on the front. What had surprised Kirsty more, was that both hers and Iain's names were written on the envelope.

Much later that night, they had opened the letter. When Kirsty's tears were blurring the words, Iain had taken the note from her and read:

Our dearest children.

If you read this letter, it means two things. One that neither of us is here anymore and two, we achieved in death what we couldn't succeed while we were alive, and that is to bring you two together. It had been our wish for years you should meet because we were convinced that you belonged together.

If we had tried to play matchmaker, you might have thought Drew was an interfering parent and I an even more interfering old grandfather, but we hoped for all these years that one day you would meet and fall in love. You guessed right. We've both have written our wills in such a way that a meeting between you might be possible—that was if we couldn't manage it before. Since you're reading this letter, it has worked.

We want you both to know that we are happy with your union and that you have our blessings. Our wish for you is to have just as happy a marriage as we both had with our wives and that your lives would be long and prosperous.

We love you, Iain and Kirsty.

Both Joe Brown and Drew Young had signed the letter, almost six months before Drew's death.

Kirsty still remembered Iain's flush when she asked, confused, "I don't understand. When have they tried to get us together?"

He had then admitted, "Sorry, Love. I think it might've been my fault. My Dad had tried several times to set me up with eligible women, and after the first time, I've dodged his attempts. You remember that woman we met in the pub in South Queensferry who gave you such dirty looks?"

When Kirsty had nodded, Iain said, "That was her. She put me off blind dates forever. I now wish I'd known it was you he'd tried so hard for me to meet the last few years."

Iain had taken another letter out of his pocket and said, "Dougie gave this to me earlier. It's quite a long letter, and you'd need to read it yourself, but the gist of it is much the same as this one. My father also explained in the letter the significance of the building and its name. You will love the story of how he and my mother met in that same building when he was still doing his articles, and she was a secretary. It was a law office then. He had already started negotiations to buy the building when she passed away."

When he had noticed the tears glistening in Kirsty's eyes, he put the letters away and took her in his arms, "Enough of the crying, Mrs Young. Let's celebrate," he had grinned.

Before Kirsty could tell him they've celebrated enough for one night, he had picked her up and carried her to bed, showing her what kind of celebrating he had in mind.

Not that she complained.

. . .

Iain's whispered, "Good morning, Mrs Young," brought Kirsty out of her musings. She lifted her hand to his cheek and whispered back, "Good morning, my Love."

Iain smiled and kissed her. He pulled back and leaned away from her. When he turned back, he had taken a document out of the drawer of the bedside table and handed it to her.

"Merry Christmas."

Kirsty opened the document, and her eyes misted over. It was the forms to register Cairistìne Court in both their names. Iain had promised it as a wedding present, but Kirsty hadn't expected him to do it so soon.

"It's not official yet, but Graeme will lodge it on the first business day," Iain explained.

Kirsty leaned in and kissed him through her tears. "Thank you."

When Iain wanted to deepen the kiss, Kirsty pulled back and smiled. "I have something for you too."

Kirsty leaned back and took something out of the drawer of the bedside table on her side of the bed. When she turned, she held out the home pregnancy stick to him, revealing the two pink lines, confirming that their little family would grow sooner than they had expected. Iain's eyes widened in surprise, and then he smiled the most beautiful smile Kirsty had ever seen. He laughed, "We're going to have a baby?"

Kirsty nodded, dropping the document and the pregnancy stick onto the bedside table before she turned to face her husband again. Iain didn't give her a chance to settle. He pushed her back against the pillows and claimed her mouth.

When he moved over her, Kirsty protested, "We have to get up. We have guests."

But Iain vetoed that. "They can wait. We still have time for this."

His eyes held hers when he filled her, his fingers entwined with hers on both sides of her face. Kirsty blamed the pregnancy hormones when her eyes misted up when he whispered, "I love you, *mo leannan.*"

THE END

ACKNOWLEDGMENTS

I will be remiss if I don't thank my family and friends for their support.

I also need to thank my beta readers, who suffer through my first drafts.

A special thank you to Sarah Bullen, the Writing Room for her support and guidance;

Editor: CA Els

Sonja Sims from Simo's Coffee Roasters in Pretoria

The Scots Language Centre

ABOUT THE AUTHOR

Romance author Francine Beaton published her first romance novel—a contemporary sports romance called EYE ON THE BALL—in April 2018 after she first started writing in July 2016. Francine calls Pretoria home, but she loves travelling to faraway places and considers Scotland her second home. When she's not reading or writing about love and Happily Ever After, she's most likely busy painting or taking photos of everything that catches her eye. During rugby season, you'll know where to find her. It will either next to the pitch or in front of the television, following her favourite teams. It's probably not difficult to figure out why her debut novel, Eye on the Ball, as well as the series, Playing for Glory, has rugby as a theme.

Receive my Newsletter

- facebook.com/FrancineBeatonAuthor
- twitter.com/BeatonFrancine
- instagram.com/francinebeaton
- amazon.com/Francine-Beaton/e/B07BJH92HR
- bookbub.com/authors/francine-beaton
- goodreads.com/goodreadscomfrancinebeaton

WOULD YOU LIKE TO LEAVE A REVIEW?

Did you like this book? If you did, I would appreciate it if you can leave a review.

BB bookbub.com/books/taste-for-coffee-taste-for-love-1-by-francine-beaton

ALSO BY FRANCINE BEATON

PLAYING FOR GLORY SERIES
Eye on the Ball (Playing for Glory, Book 1)
Obstruction (Playing for Glory, Book 2)
Leading from the Front (Playing for Glory, Book 3)
Playing by the Rules (Playing for Glory, Book 4)
Concussion (Playing for Glory, Book 5)
Wrecking Ball (Playing for Glory, Book 6)

KICK-OFF TRILOGY
Making the Right Call (Kick-Off Trilogy, Book 1)

ON THE SIDELINES SERIES
Choices (A Stand-alone Novella)

TASTE FOR LOVE SERIES
Taste for Coffee (Taste for Love, Book 1)
Taste for Wine (Taste for Love, Book 2)
Taste for Cupcakes (Taste for Love, Book 3)

BLUE MOUNTAIN SERIES
Summertime Blue (Blue Mountain, Book 1)
My Blue Heaven (Blue Mountain, Book 2)
Kind of Blue (Blue Mountain, Book 3)

THE HOPE SERIES
A Ray of Hope (Hope Series, Book 1)

www.ingramcontent.com/pod-product-compliance
Lightning Source LLC
Chambersburg PA
CBHW061220170626
46809CB00007B/2538